MORE STORIES FROM HOME

MORE STORIES FROM HOME

Judy McConnell Steele

Tamarack Books, Inc.
Boise, Idaho
1993

More Stories from Home consists of material originally published as the author's newspaper columns. Some of the material has been revised for book publication. Columns are reprinted by permission of *The Idaho Statesman*.

Cover design by Gail Ward

Cover photograph by Tom Shanahan.

Printed and bound in the United States of America.

Published by
Tamarack Books, Inc.
PO Box 190313
Boise, ID 83719-0313
1-800-962-6657, 208-387-2656, FAX 208-387-2650

To my family,

who gave me their stories and helped me tell mine.

CONTENTS

WELCOME TO THE NINETIES

Power-Camping

I might as well just tell you this straight out. I haven't got what it really takes to make it in the outdoors these days.

Last week, for example, I planned to go camping in McCall with a bunch of girlfriends.

I was really excited about the adventure. It's been a while since I've gone camping. In fact, I'm not sure if my little tent even fits me anymore.

Anyway, I was all set to go—sleeping bag, long johns, snacks, scary bedtime stories.

Then it started raining. I tried rebuilding the trip in my mind. Okay, take your heavy slicker gear. The stuff you use kayaking. Oh wait. You don't kayak.

Well, be sure and pack your fold-up shovel to dig a trench around the tent. And don't forget the waterproof matches. The ones you never bought.

After a day of internal sniveling, I called Shore Lodge and booked a room.

I guess I'm not a true outdoor girl. Don't get me wrong. I love the out-of-doors. I was excited to move to Idaho because it has so much of it. But, after getting here I discovered that being out in it isn't enough.

You have to be out doing something. And not just anything, either. The right things.

You can't just take a hike, like I used to do all the time with my family. Now you have to carry a sixty-pound pack filled with survival gear and discover a new overland route to the Yukon. Otherwise, you're only out for a sissy walk and it doesn't count.

You can't throw your tent in the Chevy and head into the mountains for a weekend camping trip.

We used to do that every Friday night my father wasn't needed at work on Saturday. Now that's called "car camping" and you'd better say it with a sneer on your lips or you're not really a child of the wilds.

Floating down a lazy stream in an inner tube isn't something to mention in outdoor circles either. Unless you like being laughed at. The only way to approach water is with a paddle in hand, a grimace on your face and a steely determination to find white water or die trying.

The way I grew up camping, water was for wading and for skipping rocks. We didn't have paddles and we didn't wear helmets. We didn't have any fancy gear at all. We didn't even have a floor in our tent.

We had no backpacks. The first hike I went on, when I was several months old, my father tied me to his back with a tea towel. It sounds like kiddy torture, but I'm grinning in the pictures.

The camp photos also reveal a lot of sitting around—around the campfire, around the picnic table and, in my brother's case, in any available dirt.

I myself preferred to sit around with a book. I shouldn't admit that now, though.

Sitting around, especially to read, doesn't score big on the outdoor charts. You should be throwing your light-weight backpacking Frisbee to your dog or lifting logs or something.

Last week, I finally had to admit to myself that my version of "Girl in the Woods" wasn't going to hit the cover of *Out-*

door Life. Worse, I had to admit it to my friends, a group of real outdoor women.

When I told them I had a dry room at the inn, they all cheered. Then they all moved in with me.

Maybe the test of a true outdoor woman is knowing when to come in from the rain.

Flashing Blades

Call me wild. Call me impetuous. Call me when I recover.

Actually, I'm feeling pretty good considering my recent encounter with a pair of in-line skates.

It all started when a friend tied on a pair of the new-fangled blades and went out for a spin. After doing the splits for the first time in her life, she decided to take a lesson. I was dragged along for comic relief.

Believe me, I wasn't picturing myself as the Chevy Chase of the blading set. I was sure I would be transformed into an instant Brian Boitano.

The idea wasn't completely farfetched. I grew up skating. This, of course, was back in the prehistoric days when a roller skate was four rusty wheels and two clamps you cranked down with your skate key.

I also know how to ice skate. Once I did an arabesque on purpose.

"This will be a snap," I told myself as I tightened up my boots for my first blading lesson. Then I tried to stand up.

Well, it had been a little while. Besides, I was weighed down with padding on most of my moveable parts.

Good thing, as it turned out.

I minced my way out to the middle of the parking lot where my instructor, Tony, stood bravely waiting for me. Other students were already practicing stops and turns.

"You ice skate?" Tony asked.

He sounded doubtful. I decided he couldn't believe a little ice skating could make me so graceful on blades.

I took off for a spin around the lot. My glides were definitely attracting attention. I heard gasps behind me.

I turned to see who was awestruck and suddenly attempted a back flip. I almost made it.

After a few more rounds, mostly standing up, I decided I was ready for the old turn stop.

This move is exactly the same as an ice skating stop. You point your feet out, carve a circle and come to a graceful halt.

I always ended my ice skating stop by standing on the tips of my blades before pushing off again. It was lovely.

I attempted a turn stop. It was fabulous.

I waited until everyone else in the class had a good view and then pulled off my second perfect stop. Anticipating the applause, I finished by standing on the tips of my blades. There were no tips, only two stupid little wheels.

I executed a perfect three-point belly landing. No one applauded. Never one to let reality discourage me, I climbed back on my skates and took a few more spins around the lot.

"Not bad," I told myself. "Not bad at all."

I was heading back to my car when Tony stopped me.

"You planning to skate again?" he asked.

"Yup," I said, sure he was going to tell me I could go directly into competition.

"Next time," he said, "try putting your knee pads on right side up."

Good Riddance

I don't miss the '80s. How could I when I never was a full member of the decade?

One day shortly after the '80s started, I mentioned in a conversation that I had been in the Peace Corps. A friend, younger than I, said, "Yeah, and then you went to work for Mother Teresa."

Even that swift kick failed to propel me into the Age of Greed.

I did make a few brave stabs at it. I learned how to vegetate on my couch in front of my VCR. I bought a pasta machine, but left it in the box.

I forgot to buy a trash compactor, a fax machine, a microwave, or a document shredder. I allowed a CD player and a personal computer to enter my house. But I created no computer viruses.

I didn't adopt a Cabbage Patch doll. I was bad at Trivial Pursuit, worse at video games.

Children of the '80s found me hopeless. I couldn't recognize He-Man or Teenage Mutant Ninja Turtles.

I didn't fit in with some adult heroes of the age either.

I didn't negotiate a merger or engineer a hostile takeover. I didn't buy junk bonds. Black Monday affected me personally only because it was my brother's birthday.

I wasn't elected, indicted or convicted. I didn't join AA, the CIA, the IRA, or the NRA.

I didn't Norville anyone out of a job. I wasn't recruited by a headhunter. I didn't turn in my urine at work.

I didn't go on "Wheel of Fortune." I didn't hit David Letterman or Geraldo. I didn't party at the Berlin Wall or discuss detente with Gorby. I didn't attend the Harmonic Convergence or go on a drug raid with Nancy.

I didn't make it burn, go the limit, or look out for number one. I didn't take steroids or have liposuction. I did try pumping iron, but only because my doctor made me.

I wasn't a surrogate mother, stay-at-home dad, or runaway child. My picture wasn't printed on a milk carton.

I didn't spot Elvis in Toledo or write a book about people who did. I didn't sleep with an evangelist or write a book about being a former sinner.

I didn't do cocaine. I didn't lose my home or my farm. I didn't contract AIDs, have an abortion, or bomb an abortion clinic. I wasn't a victim of domestic violence. I was not a terrorist or a rebel.

I didn't create a toxic waste dump, but I didn't clean one up either. I didn't save the whales. I sent them money and hope it was used wisely.

I spent much of the '80s feeling frustrated and angry over world events, but found personal happiness. So maybe I was a part of the Greed Decade.

As all greedy children discover, the '80s did not satisfy me. I want more for the world—for its people, its land, its future. It's a future I hope to find in the '90s.

Mother of All Confessions

I have a confession to make. I'm getting really tired of all these confessions.

I know, I know. It's hard to imagine that the Queen of Confessions is reprimanding other people for baring their souls. I am, after all, the person who has admitted to a secret love of napping, an addiction to chocolate, and an incessant itch to eavesdrop.

But you'll never see me talking about my family skeletons or my sex life on "Donahue."

The people clamoring to tell their lurid stories on daytime talk shows are beyond even my need to tell all.

Okay, some of them have an obvious ploy. They want to get back at an ex-spouse, a boss, or Mommy. Or they want the world to know how special they are.

Like the line-up I caught on "Geraldo" not long ago. (Yes, I confess I watch this stuff, but only when I'm too sick to change the channel.) Geraldo had gathered a group of gorgeous men and women to talk about the angst of being "Too Beautiful."

But the couple who showed up on "Oprah" one day were beyond special. They were downright scary. They were taking up air time, and my sickbed, because she had tried to kill him. Several times.

She'd just gotten out of the pen that day. And he was there to pick her up, whisk her to Oprah's show, and tell the world that he was taking her back.

Oprah asked him, "Are you going to sleep tonight?"

I wanted to ask Oprah, "Where do you find these people?"

But the most recent group I saw was the worst. A friend flipped on "Sally Jessy Raphael" just as a pretty girl appeared with the label, "Can't get prom date."

It was obvious she wanted to die. I wanted to die for her. But there was her mother, gussied up like it was her prom night, enjoying notoriety at her daughter's expense.

That mother made me realize why I'm bothered by our need to confess. It's not just that we're doing it on national TV. It's that we have to have a big problem or we're not part of the human race.

People used to ask, "Who's your family?" Now they want to know, "What's your dysfunctional family really like?"

If you won't rattle off a list of crises you've had and support groups you're attending, you're considered standoffish.

I know real people have real problems. Getting help for those problems is healthy. So is sharing them with a good friend. But I don't feel like ripping open my heart every time I meet someone.

Which is exactly what some people demand these days.

First, they want to know everything, and I mean everything, about you. If you try to accommodate them, you end up feeling like you've sold a piece of your soul. If you decline the invitation to spill your guts, they tell everyone, "She's in denial."

These folks also want to return the favor by sharing every embarrassing secret they've ever had. The truth-telling is always followed by, "Promise you won't tell anyone."

So you get to walk around saddled with the inner life of a person you barely know.

Nobody likes sharing a good story or a good cry with a friend better than I do. But, I have to confess, I'd rather skip the rest of the soul-searching admissions.

And that's the last confession I'll make. At least for a while.

Cooking for Life

The researchers are at it again.

This time, those snoopy people with the microscopes trained on our lives have decided that we all need a cooking class.

According to a recent survey by Kraft Company, people nowadays don't know their saute from their sushi. After making practical suggestions about short recipes for today's harried cooks, the study turns snotty. It says people today are unfamiliar with many cooking terms, such as "saute," "fold," and "blend."

We're talking Kraft here. These are the same guys who bring us dinner in a box. So, I'm not sure where they get off criticizing us for our lack of culinary literacy.

As far as I know, everybody is familiar with the cooking terms needed for Kraft mac and cheese. It does not take a degree from Chef Bouillabaisse's Culinary Institute to follow instructions like: Rip off box top and dump in pan.

Then, after telling us we're all gourmet illiterates, the Kraft people go and blame it on the poor schools.

"People aren't learning the cooking basics in high school like they used to," they sniff.

Face it, guys. The schools are still doing the best they can. But the last thing most fourteen-year-olds are worried about is the fine distinction between folding and blending. Unless "mixing" refers to a skateboarding maneuver, the kids don't want to hear about it.

They never did.

I remember my own intro to kitchen delights as a hotshot eighth-grader. It was not, I'm happy to tell the Kraft folks, the highlight of my cooking career. I have not started any major fires since.

My teacher, I must admit, was not the kind of whiz that Kraft has in mind for us cooking idiots. This woman actually told us, a pack of hormonally unbalanced teenagers, that we should go easy on her.

"Never, never climb up on a counter, girls," she said with a straight face. "I fell off and landed on my head."

It soon became painfully obvious that she wasn't exaggerating.

The first week, we learned about aprons. The second week, she divided us up into the six kitchen stalls and we tried to boil water.

While the water was busy boiling, we discovered we could crawl through the cupboards and visit friends in other kitchens. The teacher never did figure out how ten girls could suddenly pop up in one kitchen.

The next couple of weeks, we learned how to set fires. It wasn't on our addled teacher's syllabus, but stomping out flaming potholders and burning wastebaskets became a routine kitchen exercise.

For our last lesson, we watched while the teacher, ragged beyond belief, tried to add enough flour, eggs, and sugar to a cookie recipe to make up for the three cups of salt we'd dumped in by accident.

The next semester, the poor woman lit a match in a gas oven that had been left on by a student from the previous class. She was last seen, without eyebrows, leaving school in a hurry.

As she fled the premises, we learned a few culinary terms even the Kraft folks don't know.

The Numbers Game

"What's your number?"

The question has replaced "What's your sign?" as the hottest way to start a conversation. We're not talking income here, we're talking cholesterol level.

Singles are using the handy number to judge possible mates. Is he really fit or just looking good? Can she cook without killing me?

Friends are throwing it out as a competitive maneuver. "I'm lower, therefore I'm better."

Married couples are putting their entire relationship on the cholesterol line. "Hit 210 and I call the lawyer."

It's time for a little common sense.

I agree that we need to watch what we eat. I know fat is bad and oat bran is good. Anything that tastes like bran has to be good for you. But, as usual, we're taking a sensible rule of health and turning it into a national obsession.

A woman I know says she has friends who have become skeletal recently.

She was thinking dread diseases. Then she discovered they were trying to get healthy with no-cholesterol diets of their own devising.

The same woman says that another friend, on a similar diet, has stopped traveling.

She used to live for new sights, new thoughts, new tastes. Now she's worried she won't be able to find a restaurant with the right kind of food. So she stays home.

She's not only missing out on some great traveling, she's missing the whole point.

Health and fitness are not an end in themselves. Getting in shape is a good idea. But if all you're doing is getting in shape to stay in shape, you'll probably end up bored or so frustrated that you drop the whole thing.

Health and fitness are just a way to help us live a good life. Instead, we're running from one diet and fitness craze to another, leaving no time to enjoy our health.

Or we're doing nothing for fear it might interfere with our health regime.

We're also hanging on to our magic cholesterol number, as we have with so many good health tips in the past, as a guarantee.

"If I just stay below 200, nothing bad will happen to me."

I'm sorry to have to say it, but life isn't like that. There are no guarantees.

My grandmother had high cholesterol from the first time she was tested, in her seventies, until she died at ninety-eight.

On the other hand, a friend of mine recently suffered a stroke. She has no history of medical problems. She has low blood pressure and a low cholesterol level. She's thirty-nine.

She's used the experience to re-evaluate what is important in her life. She's making some major changes.

It shouldn't take a medical catastrophe to force us into thinking about priorities in our lives. We should know.

And we shouldn't be willing to sacrifice everything important for the sake of a number. Life is worth more than that.

Computer Error

Just as we're heading for the twenty-first century, I'm being dragged into the twentieth.

I'm now the shakily proud owner of a personal computer. Not a big deal to you, maybe. But you have to remember I'm the one who has no microwave, no fax machine, no camcorder.

I just sort of learned how to put our VCR on timer after having it twelve years.

Nevertheless, I went into the computer venture supremely confident that I was more than computer literate. I have, after all, used a newsroom computer for fifteen years and only taken the system down a few times.

I figured this new baby would be no match for my laser brain.

Some small voice of reason (probably my husband) did make me call my friend Pat the software wizard to help me set up my new home toy.

For a while, everything seemed good. Pat fed my machine its quota of floppy doo-hickeys. It blinked on and let me play a few games of Solitaire.

Then it lost its mind.

When Pat and I sat down a few weeks later to load in its new writing program, my computer said sadly that it couldn't find anything we'd fed it. It had no memory, no brain, nothing.

Pat had never seen anything like it. I started sweating, so Pat went home.

Computer cockiness draining fast, I called the technical folks at my computer place. I got Beth.

"We'll just walk you through it," she said, soothingly.

"You mean, you're going to tell me over the phone what to do?"

My voice, I noticed, was rising. I didn't sound like a computer genius. I sounded like an idiot with a machine that was laughing at me.

"You're not stupid," Beth said.

Then she started telling me, very slowly, what buttons to push to get my computer's brain back in gear.

Beth was thorough, but her plan didn't work. She thought a minute, then said, "Have you got a Phillips screwdriver?"

Words I never hoped to hear from a computer tech.

"We're going in?" I croaked.

"Sure. We need to see if your battery's unplugged or if you have a virus."

I did feel a little feverish as I searched my shelf for a screwdriver. I found a few paper clips, a leather punch, and, unbelievably, a Phillips screwdriver.

I managed to get the right screw out of the computer and the lid off. Then I stared with horror into the innards of my machine. Beth was calm.

"Look for the little black box attached to the silver box."

I followed her instructions with shaking hands. All I wanted was a writing machine. Now I was suddenly in the middle of brain surgery.

In the end, Beth decided to send over a repairman. He took one long look and declared my battery shot. The battery was replaced. My computer sprang back from the dead, full of programs and ready to write.

I'm not writing on it just yet. But I'll be using it any day now. Honest. Just as soon as I remember where I left my computer confidence.

Dating Delusion, Part I

Want proof that the world has gone mad? Several people now claim that dating is fun.

You heard me right. Some intelligent-looking human beings are using the D-word in mixed company.

These deluded souls, obviously the victims of date overload, say that the way to get romance into your life is to date. I say

it's a good way to bring misery upon your head and a plague
on your house.

Let me make myself clear. I love going on dates now. But
I get to go out with my husband.

This means I can enjoy my dinner without worrying that
something icky is sticking on my face. Or that I'll be stuck
with the bill.

I can go out knowing that we're not going to look like the
odd couple—me in a silk dress and him in well-used sweats.

I can talk about world events without wondering if he's
going to announce loudly, as one date did, "You're screwy."

I can talk about world events instead of having to answer
first date questions: What's your name again? What's your fat
intake? Where's your burial plot? What's your hurry?

I can have a good time with a handsome guy and not worry
that I'll never see him again. And we can decide, at the last
moment, to forget the date and stay home in our jammies.

To get to this blissful state, those of us in steady relation-
ships did have to become veterans of the dating wars. I myself even went out on a few dates with my future husband.

But he was my reward for an earlier date from hell.

This first date, arranged by a woman I thought was a friend,
was with Skippy the Cop.

Skippy was a new initiate on the Chicago Police Force. He
was pretty full of himself. He said, right off the bat, "Big
night, baby. I'm not wearing my guns." The date went down-
hill from there.

At the blessed end of that endless evening, I told him I
didn't want to even remember him, much less go out with

him again. He tried to give me a ticket for having a tail light out. I hope I ran over his foot.

The next day, I told my former friend that if I ever decided to date again, she owed me a big one.

She came through with the man I ended up marrying. It was the least she could do, under the circumstances.

I wish I could offer solace to everyone still out there in the dating cold. I wish I could say that things have changed.

But judging from recent war stories coming back from the dating front, the battle is still fierce.

I do have one piece of advice to pass on, however, from a sane person covering the dating skirmishes.

Alice Steinbach of the *Baltimore Sun* says we could probably cut the divorce rate in half by making married people go out once a year with strangers.

If they had to go out with Skippy the Cop, we could probably say good-bye to divorce altogether.

Dating Delusion, Part II

So who'd you wake up with this morning?

If you're like me, you aren't planning to spend Valentine's Day with any of the top ten fantasy lovers.

According to the poll in the new Harlequin Romance Report, the top ten male fantasy dates are Tom Selleck, Robert Redford, Kevin Costner, Mel Gibson, Tom Cruise, Andy Garcia, Denzel Washington, Alec Baldwin, Nick Nolte, and Luke Perry.

The top fantasy females are Cindy Crawford, Michelle Pfeiffer, Sharon Stone, Julia Roberts, Candice Bergen, Geena Davis, Kim Basinger, Whitney Houston, Winona Ryder, and Annette Bening.

Okay, cry your little heart out if you want. I know you're eyeing the lump in bed next to you, hair sticking out or maybe disappearing, and wondering where your dream mate went.

I have news for you. You've probably gotten the better deal.

Those hot dates can be cold as ice. Nothing worse than spending an endless evening with someone who only has eyes for his or her own gorgeous face.

Better to spend eternity with someone who thinks you look swell even if you've got the sniffles and are slumping around in some ratty old PJs.

On my second date with the man who became my husband, I took the plate of food I had just been served in a nice restaurant and dumped it into my lap.

"Don't worry," my future husband said. "You look good in anything you eat."

That's my idea of the perfect mate.

So is the person who remembers your birthday after only a few thunderous hints and figures out you really do want a fuss made when you protest that you don't.

Perfect mates don't take you for granted when you need to feel special. They also let you coast a little, instead of analyzing every move you make, when the rest of life gets overwhelming.

They talk when you need to talk, or at least try to. They listen, without hiding behind the paper or the dirty dishes, when you want to tell them something serious.

They think your childhood stories are cute. They've got a great sense of humor and think you do, too.

They let you be you, even when you aren't sure who that is. They play your music some of the time, go to the movie you choose once in a while.

They know how to discuss the three biggies—money, the in-laws and the kids—without flinching.

They know how to argue instead of running away. And they don't hit below the belt. No lowdown, mean arguments that bring up which one of you is getting fat and which one is looking old.

They know how to say, "I'm wrong." They know how to say, "You're right."

They're willing to show that they're in this relationship for the long haul, that little bumps might make them mad or upset but won't make them walk.

And sometimes when you least expect it, they even remember to be romantic.

The Plane Truth

A drum roll, please. The experts have another terrific announcement to make.

This time, they've decided that airplane travel is still a little too civilized. So they're going to make sure that in the future we all lose our last shred of dignity and most of our luggage by cramming more people into each plane.

According to a recent article, "long-range thinkers at Boeing and McDonnell Douglas are looking at plans for planes that seat 600 passengers or more."

Great idea, guys. Then there will be more people whining at harried airport ticket agents when the weather turns nasty and flights are scrapped. We can meet even bigger crowds of harassed, sweaty folks than I did one year trying to get home from Christmas vacation.

The whole thing started when my husband and I flew into the Salt Lake airport and found a friendly "Cancelled" sign next to our Boise number.

We didn't have to suffer alone. People had come from around the world to share this moment.

Soon my husband and I, along with sixty new friends, stood waiting with desperation in our little hearts as four ticket clerks did their best to get us home.

The man at the front of my line had missed a connection to Cairo, Egypt. The tour guide in the next line was trying to get twenty-three people, including several in wheelchairs, to Miami to meet a cruise ship. The guy right in front of us was trying to get back to Manchester, England.

He was unraveling fast, but he didn't know the worst of it. There was a big wad of toilet paper stuck to his shoe. He noticed it after the rest of us had been staring at it for a while.

His moment in the spotlight of embarrassment was eclipsed only seconds later. A man in the back of my line suddenly held up what looked like a dead rat.

"Grab the guy in the blue jacket," he yelled across the terminal. "He dropped his hair piece."

Mr. Blue Jacket, sporting a red face and a bald noggin, scurried over for his rug while the rest of us pretended not to look.

After an hour and a half of this fun, we had a new departure time—dependent on weather conditions, of course—and a seven-hour wait.

I read an entire book. I watched all my new friends eat frozen yogurt. I looked at the snow and the people piling up in the airport.

We were supposed to board at 9:12 p.m. We boarded at 10 p.m. Then we sat by the runway for two and a half hours. Various announcements were made. We were unloading some of our fuel. We were waiting for other planes to be de-iced. We were waiting, they told us, for ice cubes for our drinks.

The third seat in our row was occupied by a mother with a toddler. The poor kid was alternately laughing and crying, which is exactly the way I felt.

At 12:30 a.m., we finally took off. We got home at 3.

Next time I decide to fly in the winter, I'm going to invite a few of the swell guys calling for bigger planes. I want them along for this party they're planning.

Work, Work, Work

My friend Becky started the whole thing. By walking into the newsroom looking fabulous.

Turns out she's been spending a lot of time with Cindy Crawford. Not the actual model, just her new exercise tape.

"It works," Becky said.

I'd like to say I remained calm, counseled my aging self against anything rash.

Hah. I grabbed Cindy's "Shape Your Body Workout" and ran to my VCR. Visions of perfection danced in my head. Dance, as it turned out, was the last thing Cindy had in mind for my poor body.

Work, work, work. That's what the model and her diminutive Nazi of a trainer decided my hips, thighs, and other parts too sore to mention all needed.

I am no stranger to pain. I have been working out faithfully for at least four months now. Except for short breaks from my rigorous routine—for Thanksgiving, Christmas, the flu, and weekends—I turn on my TV at eight every morning and exercise with Amy Esterhay.

Amy is the breezy exercise hostess of Channel 4's "Homestretch." She knows her stuff. And she is toned, people, toned in places I didn't even know a weight would fit.

But she's also folksy. She tells us to pretend we're swimming through peanut butter. She says, "Whooo! We've got to get our breath here." She even sweats.

I knew Cindy wouldn't sweat. I thought I was prepared for her.

I purchased hand weights, sure that Cindy wouldn't approve of the soup cans I was using with Amy.

And I upgraded my attire. Instead of my husband's old gym shorts, which Amy usually gets, I put on a leotard topped with a sweatshirt from my twenty-fifth reunion.

"Even Cindy doesn't have one of these," I thought.

She certainly doesn't. What she does have on her ridiculously young body is legs up to her armpits. They seem to be attached with rubber bands.

She flung them around for a while, me gamely trying to follow without throwing my back out. Then she announced it was time for—groan—push-ups.

By the time Cindy and I got to "everyone's favorite, abdominals," I'd kind of lost interest. Not my mind, just what was left of my twenty-fifth-reunion body.

I returned to comfy old Amy for a few days. My spirits revived, if not my abs. I decided to try another tape. This time I turned to someone more my own age—Cher—and her new "Body Confidence" tape.

Cher, wearing a black garter belt and a web covering bitty parts of her unbelievable body, showed me how to Hot Dance. This, as it turned out, is more my style. We even did the Pony.

When the Hot Dance was over, we did some resistance training with Cher's stretchy Mighty Bands. That was when I learned that this lady might say she's my age, but she can do more slow push-ups than General Colin Powell.

After Mighty Bands, I decided to go back to the peanut butter swim with Amy. Maybe I can use my new exercise tapes as weights.

Mail-Order Love

As soon as I heard about Thomas Hoffmann, I knew, "There, but for the love of a good mother, go I."

Hoffmann was the guy who ordered about $200,000 worth of stuff from catalogs in what was described as "a mail-order frenzy."

Police said that the man's house and two storage rooms had enough loot to nearly fill an 8,000-square-foot postal service warehouse.

The sixteen policemen who spent six hours sorting through his haul found books, magazines, clothes, compact discs, globes, videotapes, and that mark of the truly crazed mail-order junkie, porcelain plates.

I haven't been reduced to ordering Norman Rockwell or Elvis plates yet. But I've come close. I've come close.

Some people love seeing their children's faces at the window when they arrive home. Others are cheered by the sight of a faithful dog dashing across the lawn to greet them.

My heart leaps at the sight of a brown parcel, large or small, sitting on my doorstep. Christmas has arrived in August. All's right with the world.

Hope rises within me just seeing the brown United Parcel truck.

Remember the children in "Music Man" singing their little lungs out about the Wells Fargo Wagon? That's me when the UPS truck rolls into view.

But I don't even have to order something to get excited. The catalogs themselves set me drooling.

I don't care if it's Neiman Marcus or Lillian Vernon. I can always spot at least one thing I can't live without.

If I give myself a few days to cool off, I usually find that the desired item has lost some of its sparkle. But, in true "mail-order frenzy," I sometimes order with abandon.

Most of my purchases are cheap but, at least in my mind, fairly tasteful. But I have been known to order silly games and worse.

I even ordered something once from Harriet Carter, the catalog with the whoopee-cushion mentality.

My item was mild—a baby's bib that said, "Kiss me, I'm Irish." But I thought the UPS man looked at me a little strangely when I signed for the package.

I know people can suffer worse than a lapse in taste when it comes to mail orders. I've heard the stories about folks being burned.

But I can't help feeling the mail-order people are my friends. They pick out presents for me and then send them right to my house. They know what I want before I do.

So I'll keep on ordering, confident that I'll never end up like Thomas Hoffmann. Because I know where to draw the line. At the Elvis porcelain plates.

THOUGHTS ON KIDS

Christmas Baby

Christmas came early for me this year.

Her name is Morgan; she weighs six pounds, twelve ounces; and she was born last Wednesday.

She's my niece, my first. I can't help feeling that, in this season of promise and light, she's coming into the world at the right moment. Her arrival has made me look back with joy and forward with hope.

When I first heard I was going to be an aunt, I started thinking about my own Aunt Mary and the special relationship the two of us had.

When I was born, my father was in the service. My aunt took care of my mother and me when we came home to her house from the hospital. She fed me at night so my mother could sleep, walked me and bathed me. She had no children of her own then. I was her baby, too.

When I was six weeks old, my mother and father and I moved to Denver, hours away from my Aunt Mary. But she and I stayed close.

She made pinafores and dresses for me. She sent me cards and letters when we weren't together, played with me when we were.

As I got older, she introduced me to her world. The first time I went fishing, I was with my Aunt Mary. I caught an ugly sucker, which almost made me cry, but the rest of the day is a bright memory.

We went hunting for arrowheads together. We talked about whatever art project we were each working on—her painting, my weaving, her patchwork, my writing.

Like my parents, my aunt encouraged me in everything I tried, made me feel that I could do anything.

Because she was my aunt and not a parent, she didn't have to discipline me or worry that I was growing up right. Once, when my brother and I had bought pipes on the sly, she showed us how to crush up seed pods and smoke them.

I spent happy hours in her backyard, playing on her glider swing and learning the names of the flowers she grew.

I spent even more time at her kitchen table, listening to the women—my mother, grandmother and aunts—talking about their lives. I learned family history at that table. I learned how the women in my family viewed the world, how they saw themselves in it.

Morgan's world is not the world I was born into. She will grow up in a big city. She will face dangers I didn't even know existed when I was young.

I can't hope to shield her or her parents from those dangers. But I can wish a safe passage for all of them.

I can pray that our country will start taking care of its problems. I can hope for a society that cherishes and supports its women in all their talents the way my aunt supported me.

In some ways, I will be a different aunt to Morgan than my Aunt Mary was to me. I probably won't make her dresses. I may not get to take her fishing.

But I plan to welcome her into the world, to encourage her and be her friend. It's the best gift I can offer this Christmas baby. And it's the best gift I can receive from her.

Lost Children

Shame on us.

Idaho is last in state spending per child for preschool child care and development, fiftieth in spending per student.

We've been bickering over five million dollars in the public school budget. In the meantime, there are children in our state who are floundering. An alarming number of them are drowning.

During the 1990-91 school year, almost nine percent of our sophomores dropped out of high school. More than ten percent of the juniors and more than nine percent of the seniors left. In some communities, the dropout rate is as high as twenty-five percent per class.

Once they leave, dropouts face a bleak future.

"There's nothing out there for them," says Dean Bob Barr, dean of Boise State University's College of Education.

"The dropout will enter a growing class of young men and women who will live and die in America and never work," Barr says. "They will fall into drugs and crimes."

America is changing fast, he says. The great American dream of making something of yourself through a strong back and sheer grit is a dream lost.

The fields and forests are becoming mechanized. The factories are closing down or replacing workers with machines. The military is only looking for a few good educated men and women.

There will soon be no place for strong shoulders and an uneducated mind.

We start training dropouts early. Consider this chilling fact: The state of Indiana, Barr says, is now predicting the number of prison cells it will need in fifteen to twenty years by studying today's second-graders.

It's those children, the youngest, that we need most desperately to reach. The one consistent factor among dropouts, Barr says, is illiteracy. And most children learn to read between age three and eight or not at all.

Instead of putting the money and energy into saving young lives, we are spending it when lives are already lost.

At the same time we gave a paltry twenty-four cents per child for preschool child care and development, we spent over twenty-four times that amount on prison systems.

We respond to crime because it threatens us. But we ignore the greater crime—the waste of young minds.

We have to take our children's lives seriously. We need to reduce class sizes so children can receive more individual attention, pay good teachers the same salaries they could make in other states, develop programs and buy equipment to train students for a changing world.

We need to find more money for our children, even if it means raising taxes.

Money won't solve all of the problems facing young children, their parents and their teachers. But it will help.

In the long run, we'll save money now spent on prisons, welfare and drug programs. And we'll save children.

Young Friends

Child-free, the way to be?

Mike and Jean Carter think so. They've written "Sweet Grapes," a book on "child-free living."

The book sounds as though it has a lot of comforting and sensible advice for people who can't have children.

Like many of us who went through the traumatic "cycle of hope," the Carters finally accepted the fact that they weren't going to get pregnant. They embraced what they call a "child-free" life.

Their choice is a good one. But I'm bothered by their term "child-free."

"Childless" does sound pitiful, as if you're less than whole. But "child-free" sounds as though you work hard to stay away from kids.

It reminds me of a Miss Peaches cartoon I saw of a camp counselor. He had small fry attached by their teeth to various parts of his body. He was babbling about taking a kerosene bath.

There are kids who bring out the kerosene bath in me. But there are also children I love to see and miss when we're apart too long.

My godchild, Andrew, is one of those kids.

The night my husband and I were asked to be his godparents, baby Andrew screamed through most of dinner.

"He's disappointed," my husband joked. "He was hoping for a Rockefeller."

It's the last time he's ever acted disappointed to see us. In the four years since, we've been greeted regularly with big hugs.

We have long conversations about everything—school, new tennis shoes, his brother and sisters. They're our friends too.

My husband and I are like young grandparents. We get to spoil the kids and not pay the consequences, romp with them and then let Mom and Dad calm them down for bed.

We're there for some of their big moments—birthday parties, school plays, soccer games, ballet recitals, trick or treat. We share some of the small moments like a book and a goodnight hug.

We're not changing diapers. We're only burping the baby when we feel like it.

But we're getting to watch them grow up.

We first met these kids because their parents are our friends. Now we're developing friendships with each of them that will be separate from the relationship with their parents. We plan to be friends with them when they're adults if they want.

A colleague who has children says those friendships are special for the kids as well.

Children with grownups as friends learn there are different ways to live in the world. They discover they can visit an adult friend and survive without Mom and Dad.

They find out they can be friends with people of all ages.

Which is all I want to do. I hope always to have older, wiser friends and younger friends who can help me remember to have fun.

Child-free I will never be.

Week of the Young Child

This is the Week of the Young Child. The idea of it makes me furious.

I'm glad we have a week to think about children and the people who care for them. I'm angry that we have only a week.

We should honor children every week of the year. We should respect and cherish them.

But in this country we vacillate between worshiping children briefly and then, like sacred cows in India, leaving them to wander on their own.

There are compelling reasons that children are being left on their own.

Many parents have to work. They are alone or they are struggling even with two salaries. They are getting little or no help from a government and society that don't care whether their children make it or not.

Many parents cannot even find adequate daycare.

Almost 102,000 Idaho children up to age nine need care while their parents work. There are only 17,417 licensed spaces in the state for those children. Some of the rest stay with relatives and friends. Others are on their own.

Other basic childhood needs are not being met either.

Immunization is debated as though it were only a political issue and not an ethical decision.

Little children are going to bed hungry. In Idaho, one out of every six children under twelve lives with hunger.

Many schools and daycare centers are overcrowded and badly equipped. Teachers cannot spend much time with each child. And they are so poorly paid they often have to take second jobs or leave teaching to take care of their own families.

In the 1990-91 year, Idaho ranked forty-fifth in the nation in our pay rate for teachers. In 1991-92, we slid to forty-seventh.

Daycare workers in Idaho fare worse—most of them make less than parking lot attendants. The message is clear: We're more concerned about our cars than our children.

The people caring for children hear that message. They face a society that tells them every day that they and their children are a low priority.

That society is us. We vote for the people who decide where the money and support go, who gets the attention and who doesn't. For many years now, we've been letting parents, teachers and caregivers know that we don't value their work or the children they're raising.

Right or wrong, there are armies fighting for the rights of the unborn child. Where are the armies fighting for the rights of the children already born?

Children are crying for food, for shelter, for guidance and the comforts that this country and this state have in abundance. And we're staying silent.

Let's raise our voices high this Week of the Young Child. Let's give a glad cry for the people who are fighting for children's rights.

Then let's keep making loud noises for the sake of the children. We cannot fall silent again.

Love of Learning

When John and Valerie Charneski won over twenty-one million dollars in the Wisconsin lottery recently, Valerie knew exactly what she wanted to do with some of the money.

"I always wanted to go to college," she said. "Now I can."

Her statement lifted the hearts of some of us. Instead of cars, boats or a big house, Valerie was dreaming about going back to school.

But other people met her decision with hoots of derision. One Boise disc jockey said, "So what's she going to do with an education, earn more money?"

His comment reflects a growing assumption in this country that the only reason to go to school is to make money.

It's true that it's getting harder to make even a semi-decent living without a degree. But going to college only to increase earning potential is a sad way to look at education.

Unfortunately, kids are learning a lesson from the adults. Classes, as far as many teens are concerned, should all be job-oriented.

In a recent survey, almost 27,000 teenagers said they wanted to go to good colleges to land high-paying jobs. They also said salary was more important than career satisfaction or challenge.

A teenager named Stephanie, who's sixteen and wants to be a doctor, said, "I want to be rich . . . . I want to be rich more than anything in the world."

Despite that sentiment, these teens aren't greedy. As the survey pointed out, they're looking for security.

Stephanie went on to say, "If I were rich, it would be easier to pay the bills."

In a shaky world punctuated by the homeless, possible war, rising crime, a high divorce rate and harried parents, school kids are worried about the future.

My heart goes out to them. Despite the turmoil of the '60s and '70s, many of us grew up knowing we could try just about anything. Jobs were easy to get, money and security there if we needed them.

These kids don't have that assurance. And, in the stampede for security, they've lost more than the feeling they will be okay. They've also lost the idea that education is valuable for itself alone.

Somehow, we have to help kids understand that learning can be an exciting process of exploration. School can and should be a time of discovery as well as training. Classes should open up unknown possibilities, not just provide the next logical step in a planned life.

Learning gives life its zest, its color. Without it, we stagnate.

I don't mean teens shouldn't be given valuable work skills. Still, the best skill anyone can learn is how to learn. That can carry you through a lifetime of changes and challenges.

The kids now looking at college will probably not have one lifetime job. Most people will change jobs, even careers, several times in their lives.

But learning, as our lottery winner knows, is forever.

Christmas Kid

I'll warn you right now. I'm a fool for Christmas.

I'm the person singing along to the Muzak version of "Silent Night" in the grocery store.

I'm the one with the sloppy grin watching the Christmas tree light up. I'm the one urging everyone to have another round of eggnog.

I know, I know. It's not politically correct to be in love with Christmas. We're supposed to complain about the stress, the lines, the endless Christmas carols and purchases.

I agree that Christmas can get out of hand. At times, it's too expensive, too wasteful, with too much emphasis on buying and too little on peace and good will.

And I do take offense at any mention of fruitcake.

But I anticipate everything else about the season—singing Christmas carols, putting up decorations, going to parties, donating food and toys to collections.

I like to make cookies and candy, eat cookies and candy, visit friends and find the perfect present for someone.

I start thinking about Christmas some time in March. By June, I'm seriously thinking about presents. By October, I'm peeking into the boxes of decorations.

I'm sure my husband will never buy a fake Christmas tree. He knows I'd have it set up before Halloween.

I understand that Christmas can be a stressful time, especially for kids. I taught four- and five-year-olds. I saw kids getting wound up and tired.

But I also saw their eyes sparkle when they discovered that Santa's elves had changed their paper candy canes into real candy canes.

Some folks say that's lying.

I have friends who thought they might not tell their child about Santa. It just didn't seem truthful to them.

They soon found out that their child would have to be stashed in a dark closet to keep her from hearing about Santa.

More to the point, Santa brings magic into young children's lives. He's a wonderful friend for them.

One Christmas, another teacher and I were in the basement of the school, wrapping presents for Santa's bag, when a little boy wandered in.

We both froze, sure we'd spoiled his Christmas. But his face lit up and he said, "You're helping Santa!"

I remember the wondrous feeling as a child on Christmas Eve. I knew that Santa would find me even though I didn't have a chimney.

And I remember the year I heard that Santa was not a real person. I didn't feel cheated. I felt grown-up, in on the secret. My parents explained the spirit of Santa so gently to me that none of the magic was lost.

I know when it get further into December, I'll be a little harried, a little stressed. But I'm certain the Christmas spirit will carry me through. I hope it carries you through, too.

Let the magic sustain you.

Popsicle Thoughts

Sometimes I'm a little slow. It takes me a while to figure out why something is bothering me.

I'd been feeling that way about year-round schools.

In my head, I know year-round schools could work well. It makes sense to have the school used all year. And students taking shorter breaks don't forget as much, don't get as bored during short vacations.

But in my heart, the notion still bothers me.

It took a Popsicle truck to help me understand why I was balking at the idea.

Actually, not even the truck itself. Just its little jingle. As soon as I heard its nostalgic tune bouncing through my back yard, I realized why I didn't like year-round school.

Because my childhood summers, which the truck's song brought back to me, would not have been as wonderful if I'd gone to a school with staggered vacations.

I almost lost those summers.

When I started kindergarten, along with the rest of the early baby boomers, school officials decided to stagger the bulging numbers by having some of us start in the winter and go through early fall.

But hot June rolled around in those days before air-conditioned schools and everybody decided to reconsider. We left after six months of kindergarten and took our three full months to play Huck Finn.

During those early summers, my brother and I went swimming in the creek near our house, caught tadpoles and frogs for a trough in our back yard, crawled through the neighborhood fields of tall grass playing spy.

We swung on the swing and trapeze our dad had put up for us, played tetherball and baseball, made up new acrobatic tricks on our bikes. At night, we played kick-the-can until Mother called us in for bed.

We went to the parks for picnics, went to the library to check out stacks of books, went to movie matinees, lay around in the grass under trees.

I don't even remember getting bored much.

We took long car trips most summers. As a minister, my father worked six or seven days a week most of the year. So the church gave him four weeks of vacation every summer.

Two summers, we traded churches with another minister's family. We spent one month in Calgary, the other in a beach house near Atlantic City.

My father's vacations were longer than many people get today. My mother was home. We had no television. The world was a different place.

It started changing long before I stopped going to school. By the time I was in junior high, my mother was working. By the time I was in senior high, I was working summers.

I know that year-round school makes a lot of sense for a lot of people. I know that some children today would be stir-crazy after a month of my idea of idyllic summer.

Still, I wish there were a way to give them and all of us those summers. Summers that seemed as endless and sweet as the Popsicle man's tune.

The Working Life

School's out. Kids are grinning. Parents are groaning. What to do with the offspring all summer? I'd like to advocate summer work for kids.

Not the little ones. I'm not a big proponent of sweat shops for tiny tots. I like the idea that small children have time to lie in the grass.

Older kids, like all of us, need a little soul-gazing time as well. But they also need some time to learn about life in the working world.

I know it's not easy for somebody fourteen to get a job. I faced the same problem at that age. Thanks to adults willing to take on a slightly goofy but eager girl, I always found a job.

One summer, I took care of a little boy every morning while his mother was at work.

That summer, although I was a sophisticated fifteen, I got to go back to my own childhood for a while.

Jimmy and I set up a lemonade stand on the front sidewalk. We had shoot-outs with cap pistols while hiding behind trees in the backyard. We made model airplanes in the basement.

I hope Jimmy had a good time. I had a ball.

Another summer, I was hired to work in my father's office every morning. That was probably as long as anyone could put up with the boss's kid.

There were other jobs along the way, including a memorable spring break stint retyping university records that had grown mold in an underground storage vault. I came home every day smelling like The Swamp Thing.

The last summer before I went out into the real world of work as a college kid, I was hired to babysit a minister's office while he was away.

No one stopped by. The phone hardly ever rang. And I was surrounded by walls of bookshelves with good books. I still dream about that job.

My summer jobs, whether great or lousy, did more than expand my literary knowledge. They gave me a real education in the way the working world works.

I learned how to conduct myself in an office situation. I learned skills I still use. I learned how to work with people. I made some good contacts for future jobs and future references.

And, at least one summer, I was able to spend time with my dad.

I learned a little bit about what he did. I learned more about who he was. We came home and talked office politics. We told office jokes. We got to know each other better.

I was lucky.

A lot of kids grow up without ever seeing their parents at work. They don't know how their parents spend their days, what they enjoy about their jobs, what they don't like.

My brief moment in my father's work life was invaluable.

So was my glimpse of the working world. It gave me training for future jobs, helped me decide what I wanted those jobs to be.

I couldn't have done it without parents willing to hand over their children to me, bosses willing to trust me with work, secretaries patiently showing me for the sixth time how to use the ditto machine.

Now it's up to us. We're the parents, the bosses, the secretaries. We can open up the door and greet the next generation eager for the chance to work.

Advice from Aunt Judy

A few days ago, I called my old friend Liz.

I haven't seen her since her little boy was running around in soggy diapers. Now I find out he's off to his sophomore year of college.

After I pulled myself back from that time warp, Liz and I started talking about the day we went off to college together.

It was a different world then. When we arrived on campus, we were given class schedules, purple and white beanies, and dormitory curfews with punishments for being late.

We were young, we were naive. But we weren't totally unprepared for our adventure.

We had read *1984*, *Walden Two* and the rest of the reading list. We had picked out the cutest boys from the latest yearbook. And, along with the formals and tennis rackets, we had packed up a load of advice.

The beanies and 9 p.m. curfews have disappeared. But the advice, it seems, hasn't changed at all.

College kids today are being sent off with the same words of wisdom we heard: "Study hard;" "Don't spend too much money;" "Be careful;" "Be good."

Smart advice. But, as a former college student turned part-time adult, I'd like to add to the list.

First, I hope every college student takes a few risks. And every parent is willing to let it happen.

I'm not talking about driving Deadman's Curve after an all-night party. I'm talking about signing up for that fascinating course even if it isn't in your game plan. It may capture you and change your life.

Second, come up for air once in a while. Dad's right—you need to study hard. You also need to get out of the books occasionally.

Life is out there. This is your chance to see it without having to worry about the next meal for your family.

Third, take care of yourself. Green veggies, sleep, the things your mother told you to do. Do them. Get some fresh air. Do a few deep knee bends for those of us who can't do them any more.

Take care of the rest of yourself, too.

Find friends you can trust, professors who are on your side. You'll know them when you meet them. And you'll want to know them for the rest of your life.

Liz and I could have used some of this advice when we set off on our life adventure. Come to think of it, I could still use this advice. Except for the deep knee bends.

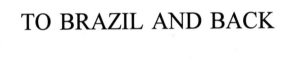
TO BRAZIL AND BACK

Ate Logo

Brazilians often say, "Ate logo." It means, "This isn't good-bye. This is just so long for a little while."

By the time you read this column I will be living in Brazil. But this is not good-bye, just "ate logo."

I plan to write my column during my two and a half months stay, to share my adventure with friends at home.

The trip is proof that dreams do come true.

The day I hugged my Brazilian friends and tearfully boarded the plane for home, I promised I would be back. That was twenty years ago. I was leaving a town called Aracaju and work with Peace Corps.

No one could have told me the first few months of my stay in Aracaju that I would be crying when I left.

When I first arrived in Brazil, I was miserable. I'd known I was going to a foreign country, but hadn't realized that nothing would be familiar.

The food was different, the vegetation was different. I looked at stars I didn't recognize in the nighttime sky. Even the air was heavier and carried smells that were pleasant but unrecognizable.

Despite several months of intensive language training, I couldn't understand a word that was said to me. My neighbors, wading bravely into my stabs at Portuguese, had the same trouble with me.

Attempting to tell one man "Good morning"—the first lesson in any language book—I came really close with a word which translates "little rear end."

Answering a friendly woman's question about what Americans eat for breakfast, I concluded not with "aveia," or oatmeal, but "areia," which is sand.

There were gaps in my cultural understanding as well. But the good-hearted Brazilians stayed with me, explained things to me.

And one day I woke up wondering how I could ever leave the country.

I did leave, but I was back two years later with Project Hope in the city of Natal. At the end of that stay, I again promised I would return.

Two years ago, my husband and I started talking about a vacation in Brazil. But I finally realized I wanted to be more than a tourist. I asked for and was granted an educational leave from the newspaper.

I plan to use some of my time to explore new territory as a volunteer with a health care organization. I also want to go back to the old places, look up friends I haven't seen in twenty years, revisit the towns where I lived.

Friends have warned me gently that my memories may be only memories now. Aracaju and Natal have grown. Friends have died or moved. I have changed.

It may be true that I can't go home again. Whatever happens, whatever changes I see or familiar favorites I rediscover, I hope to share in my column.

And so, until next week, I'll just say, "Ate logo."

Sunday in Salvador

As soon as the plane door opens, you know you're far away from home. Warm, moist air rushing in carries the aroma of sweet flowers and hot vegetation.

Salvador, Bahia, is a 300-year-old port city of a million and a half people. Home of many of Brazil's best musicians and artists, it was once the center of the slave trade and is now a rich blend of European and African cultures.

Colonial houses and churches nestle next to new high-rise apartments, small houses and open-front stores made of mud and plaster. Beaches stretch along the city's side like a sleeping sun bather.

On Sunday afternoon, most of Salvador is at the beach. But the streets of the old city, in an area called Pelourinho, are still full of people and life.

Along one street, a Bahiana woman—wearing a traditional costume of a long full skirt, an overblouse in white lace, a white scarf covering her hair and strings of beads blessed by her African gods—sells spicy food and skewers of meat she cooks on a charcoal grill set on the narrow sidewalk.

In a square with sand and palm trees, a man has set up a little stand filled with fruit he is selling. Small red bananas, one of a half a dozen varieties, lay next to pinhas, a fruit that looks like a soft hand grenade. Strollers split open the fruit with their hands and suck the meat from each large seed.

Children kick a soccer ball expertly up and down a side street. Dogs doze on the warm sidewalk. A man wearing a brown shirt and tattered shorts sleeps in a doorway. Another rides by on a bicycle with a frame made of wood. Brazilians have a saying: "If you don't have a dog, you hunt with a cat."

Laundry is strung across an iron grillwork balcony. A woman stands at another balcony, framed by arched windows with slatted wooden shutters. Below her, another woman is shuffling cards at a rickety table. Three men stand around the table, throwing down money and watching intently as she deals the cards.

Around the corner, people sit in open doorways, talking or just watching the street scene. A boy with a large oil can balanced on his head walks down the center of the cobblestone street. He is playing an intricate rhythm on a triangle to draw attention to the coconuts he's selling from the can.

Iron gates in the walls that line the street are closed, but let sunlight into small courtyards. An iron sculpture decorating one courtyard, in the former house of Brazilian author Jorge Amado, depicts the origin of Pelourinho. A slave, chained to a post, is being whipped by his master. Pelourinho—the pillory.

Iron gates protect more than courtyards. Most of the gates covering store fronts are closed on Sunday. But a few are rolled back to help shoppers see the goods inside.

One shop sells beads that are used in candomble, the African religion brought to Brazil by the slaves. Another tiny shop offers newspapers, magazines, cigarettes.

A third sells coffins. The biggest and most ornately carved coffins are propped against the wall just inside the iron gate. They are dark wood and massive. Farther back along the wall are plain, white coffins. They are reserved for young women who have not married.

Babies' coffins, also white, stand on shelves against the back wall. The store owner sits in a chair on the sidewalk, waiting for customers.

Birth to death. It's all part of life on the streets and sidewalks of Salvador.

Sea Goddess

Today I'm going to learn who my candomble god is.

My friend Paulo has promised to take me to a *mae dos santos*, a woman who practices the ancient African religion of candomble. The religion was brought to Brazil by slaves who mixed it with the rituals of the Catholic church.

It is usually not malevolent. Its gods protect people and the earth and perform good deeds.

The mae Paulo is taking me to see will conduct a ritual and then tell me which of the candomble gods and goddesses is my protector.

"I'm taking you to the house of one of the most famous maes," Paulo says. "She was over one hundred years old. She died two years ago, but other maes are there."

A young boy leads us down a hill on a narrow dirt street to a white plaster house with a columned veranda. Several sets of narrow double doors, painted sky blue, are closed.

A stone porch in the back is covered with a roof of palm fronds and lined with cages on one side. Each cage contains a chicken.

"The chickens are for sacrifices in some of the ceremonies," Paulo says.

No one is there. We head back up the hill, led by the boy and joined by a neighbor lady and several small children. They will show us where another mae lives.

She is at home—a pleasant-looking woman, in her sixties, wearing a cotton house dress.

I follow her to a back room she has prepared for the ceremony. It's a little room, just large enough for a small table and several straight-back chairs.

She closes the double doors and sits at the table, arranging statues of several Catholic saints, a white plate with a glass of water on it and strands of beads in different colors.

She moves the beads to a different position around the plate, chanting softly over them. Picking up one strand, she places it, balled in her fist, on my forehead.

Still chanting, she peers intently into the glass of water, turning it slowly.

"Your goddess is Iemanja," she says.

Iemanja, goddess of the sea. On February 2, people bring small boats filled with flowers, candles and presents to the beach and set them out on the water for Iemanja. Some who pay homage are on foot. Some are in limousines. Iemanja protects them all.

"I see only good things for you. I don't see anything bad, no illness. You and your husband are good together. You're good friends," she says.

Later, Paulo gives me beads prepared for me by a mae. They are clear with a silvery sheen—the color of Iemanja's sea.

"Most people wear them inside their shirts to protect them," Paulo says.

I tuck mine in my blouse.

I once asked a Brazilian friend—well-educated and from an upper-class family—what he thought of candomble.

"Please understand, I am a good Catholic," he told me.

Then he pulled a chain from inside his shirt. On it hung a small candomble amulet.

Going Home

Forget what you've heard. You can go home again.

It doesn't happen often. But once in a while, if you're lucky, you can walk right into your past.

When I went to Bairro America last week, the little community where I was a Peace Corps volunteer twenty years ago, I didn't expect to find anyone or anything I remembered.

A new paved road cutting through the middle of the bairro had changed everything, people said. Houses were gone; people had moved away. Even the old penitentiary, surrounded by mud houses for guards' and prisoners' families, had been torn down, they said.

And I had no hope of finding Dona Analia—my neighbor, friend and guide through the sometimes bewildering world of a poor Brazilian community those many years ago.

She was the bairro wise woman. People brought her their letters to read to them and told her their problems. She gave them advice and herbal teas when they were sick.

Early in my two-year stay in Bairro America, I was sick for several days. Nothing in my American medical kit was helping. Dona Analia picked leaves from a plant outside my door and brewed a tea. I was better in an hour, cured in a day.

She was my Brazilian mother, teaching me to talk properly, to cook, to see what was really happening in the bairro.

"Look at the animals, Judite. They're as thin as the children. That isn't right."

Other people accepted life in the bairro. She knew there was a better way to live.

I thought she had left the bairro, maybe even died. She would be in her seventies now.

I drove into the bairro, got out of the car and walked in the direction of my house. Nothing looked familiar.

I had a photograph of Dona Analia. I walked up to a group of boys and pulled out the photo. The boy nearest me glanced at the picture and said, "She's my neighbor. Her house is right up the road."

I drove up the dirt road. There, sitting in her front yard as she had twenty years ago, was Dona Analia.

We hugged, both teary-eyed. And then I found out how close I'd come to missing this moment.

"I had a stroke in January," Dona Analia told me. "I almost died."

She's still weak. But her grandson told me her mind was sharp through all of her illness.

We sat in her yard twenty years later and reminisced about all we had done together. The day she taught me to kill, clean, and cook a chicken. The coconut cakes we baked together.

Then it was time for me to leave. I promised to write, promised to come back. She hugged me one last time and said, "Deus te abencoe, Judite. God bless you, Judy."

He already has, Dona Analia. He already has.

Lists and Lines

On a typical Saturday in Boise, you and I can make a list of errands and expect to get through most of it.

In an hour or two, we've gone grocery shopping, stopped at the post office, visited the bank.

Middle-class people in Natal, Brazil, make the same lists. They jump in their cars, buy groceries, mail letters, deposit money. If they're lucky, they may get everything done in one day. But they don't count on it.

True, they're living in a city of 500,000, so stores and parking spaces are farther apart. But the little items of every-day life just consume more time.

Take food. Natal has the Brazilian version of Albertson's stores. People use them regularly. But they don't buy everything there.

Meat is available in the store, but often is better in the butcher shop several miles away. Bread is tastier from the bakery. Fruit and vegetables are fresher in the farmers' market.

If you do find good produce at the grocery store, you have to wait in one line to have it weighed. Then you stand in another line to pay for it.

In department stores, one person helps you pick out your shirt or shoes or toothpaste, then sends you with a slip to pay a cashier.

That person sends you with your receipt to a third person, who wraps your purchase. Each step involves lines of people.

In the post office, you run the same obstacle course of lines. But you have to head bravely in—letters are not picked up at people's houses.

Bills can't be mailed from home or the post office. They have to be paid at the bank, where you'll run into the longest lines of all.

Visits to businesses can be equally frustrating. Equipment breaks down. People have to close up shop to run messages when the phones refuse to work. And most stores and offices close down in the noonday heat and stay sensibly closed until midafternoon.

So middle-class people in Natal often arrive home with one item checked off their list of six errands. Once they get there though, the frustrations vanish.

Lunch is on the table, prepared by the live-in maid most middle-class families employ. She'll have the house clean as well.

The washerwoman will have washed the clothes and hung them up to dry. She'll be back later to iron.

The seamstress will stop in later as well. The gardener will be making his weekly visit. There may even be a manicurist coming in.

And friends and family will be dropping in for cups of hot, sweet coffee and good gossip.

You'll have to fit them in around an afternoon siesta in your hammock and join them for an evening of music and dancing at a beach nightclub. Which more than makes up for the hassles of the morning.

Back in Time

Traveling from city to countryside in northeast Brazil is like going backwards in time.

Many of the coastal cities are big and busy. They have big buildings, big businesses, big-city problems. But the interior, with sleepy little towns, could be the American West of a hundred years ago.

Each small town has at least one church and one bar. On Saturday, the men sit at wooden tables on the bar's veranda and drink beer or play table soccer. On Sunday, the women go to church.

Whether night falls on a day of gossip at the bar or prayer in church, families go for a stroll through the dark to visit friends or just to see everyone else who's out strolling.

Cars come by on the two-lane highway that runs through some of the towns. Few stop. Fewer belong to anyone in town. Most people use carts pulled by India cows with sad eyes and floppy ears. Or they ride horses bareback, gathering on the road to talk.

Even on weekdays, life is slower in the small towns.

Families take care of their chickens, fish in nearby rivers, tend to the youngest children and the garden. Women sit under trees with cloth stretched on wooden frames, making lacy tablecloths to be sold in the cities.

They wash clothes in the river, then hang them to dry on fences made of tall sticks bound with wire.

Health care for people with little or no money is available in the cities. You may have to wait for a long time in a crowded clinic. You may not get the best or latest treatment. But you will be taken care of.

Out here in the small places, it's not as easy. Some small towns have health posts. Many have nothing. It can be miles and hours to the nearest medical center.

But there are advantages to being in the country if you're poor. Most people can have a garden, a few chickens or a pig, a house and a hammock to sleep in. In the city, it's harder to find a place to sleep, some ground to grow vegetables.

Like small western towns in the U.S., the people in the little places make their own fun.

They have dances with bands. They make costumes for Carnival, including tall masks that look more like ceremonial headpieces than the feathered spangles of Rio's Carnival.

Sometimes, a circus arrives in town. The circuses traveling the interior are tiny. Four or five people do everything. They set up the tent and wooden benches, sell tickets and food, perform flashy juggling acts and balancing stunts.

Television has come to the small towns as well. At night, people arrange their chairs in front of an outdoor cement stand holding the town's television set. They sit in the dark, their faces lit by the screen's blue glow.

Whatever their situation, people in the small towns usually accept it. They welcome the chance to improve their lives, but they don't expect it.

After all, in Portuguese "to hope for" and "to wait for" are the same word.

Sunny Days, Rising Prices

This time of year, Brazilians used to talk about one thing—Carnival. This year, they're discussing only one thing, but it isn't Carnival. It's inflation.

"If we didn't have the inflation, we wouldn't have anything to talk about anymore," says my friend Carmelia.

She's joking, but inflation is no laughing matter here. In January, the official rate of inflation was over fifty percent. Banks are predicting that the official rate for February will be a record sixty-five percent.

Some people say that the real rate may be even higher. No one questions that it's rising swiftly. All they have to do is compare prices now to prices a month, a week, sometimes even a day ago.

Last week, a loaf of whole grain bread in one store was twelve cruzados novos. This week, it's nineteen. A mailbox Carmelia thought about buying was 710 cruzados novos.

When she went back the next day to buy it, the price was 980.

The price of gas and alcohol, which many Brazilian cars use, is going up for the third time since the beginning of the year. People heard rumors of the latest price hike and started telling each other, "Fill up your tank. The cost is going up."

Within a day, there were long lines at the gas stations. And the prices did rise.

Shoppers fight inflation by buying large quantities of non-perishable items such as soap, toilet paper and canned goods whenever they can.

One of the nightly news reports on the problem said that the lines in Rio grocery stores at the beginning of the month—when most people had just received their paychecks—were longer than the lines of cars going to the beach.

When people have extra money, they spend it. They buy dollars. They buy cars or bicycles. Or they put their money in a variety of savings plans that are supposed to compensate for the inflation.

Employers have to deal with monthly salary increases. Some of them, with minimum-wage employees running out of money by the second or third week, are letting their employees borrow against next month's salary.

People below the poverty line, those at the bottom, spend what little money they get immediately, before it devalues. They barter to make it through most of the days.

The struggle is affecting almost everyone. One friend, whose family is middle-class, notes that the summer holidays he used to enjoy with his buddies at the beach aren't the same any more.

"Nobody has any money now," he says sadly.

Everyone says something must be done and soon to push down the skyrocketing costs. The president-elect of Brazil says he has a plan to reduce inflation. But he won't talk about it until his inauguration in mid-March.

Until then, Brazilians can count on two things—days of sunshine and rising prices.

Two Loves

Hello, Boise. Bye-bye, Brazil.

Caught with one foot in each continent, I'm feeling the conflict of every traveler who's fallen in love with a foreign country.

You're happy to be home, to see your old love. You wonder why and how you ever left the new love of your life.

The mixed feelings loomed as soon as I landed in Boise.

I was greeted by a husband I missed more than I could have imagined, the smiling faces of good friends, beautiful spring weather and a longing to take them all back with me.

I miss some of the big moments I shared in Brazil.

I watched excited voters celebrating, some with tears in their eyes, during the inauguration of the first president they've elected in decades.

It was a shock to see the contrast between those hopeful citizens, talking about new freedoms, and the lethargy and cynicism that has infected our own political system.

I miss little everyday moments as well.

I'd like to get up every morning in Boise, as I did in Natal, and pick up the delicious mangoes that fell during the night.

I'd like to go on a morning walk on the beach, then take shelter from the sun in an outdoor cafe selling good shrimp and beer. I'd like to drink a cafezinho, a little cup of strong Brazilian coffee, at a sidewalk stand.

I'd like to share that coffee with someone. In Brazil, that's almost a given.

No one is ever alone unless he wants to be. And most people don't want to be. When a survey in Brazil asked people to name the last time they had been alone, most couldn't remember. Which was fine with them.

Families stay connected. Grown children drop in on their parents every day. Uncles know their nieces and nephews as well as their own children.

Families and friends show each other how they feel. They hug; they kiss. They go to parties together where three or four generations all have fun. Their houses are as open as they themselves are to anyone who drops in for a quick cup of coffee or a long talk.

Yet most of them have to live behind high walls.

Burglary is becoming a daily concern for people in all but the most remote areas. Cars are locked up even when they're in driveways. Purses are clutched tightly.

Brazilians, some of the friendliest people on earth, are learning to be wary.

I'm happy to be back in Boise, a town where I can walk down a street in daylight and not worry. A place where I can drink the water right out of the tap, where I can depend on the expertise of doctors.

This is home. My husband and some of my best friends are here. But I miss the good friends I left behind. Like anyone who's been away from home and seen another good place, a piece of me will always be in Brazil.

LAUGHING AT LIFE

Tabloid Addict

"Shocking but true. Normal-looking woman bears brunt of onlookers' scorn. Reads sleazy tabloid in front of crowd."

That woman was me. My public humiliation was, of course, in a grocery store.

Innocently walking past the checkout stand I was sucked into a headline reading: "His tongue is 8 inches long . . . and it's still g-r-o-w-i-n-g!"

Long minutes later, I came to. A voice next to me was snapping: "Are you in this checkout line or are you just reading?"

I looked up. Faces around me stared. Like the E.F. Hutton ad, everything stopped. What would I say?

"Er, reading," I admitted and slunk off to the frozen food section to avoid more sneers.

Okay, it's out. I am a tabloid junkie.

I don't just glance at headlines. Everyone does that. (Come on, 'fess up.)

No, I read whole sordid stories. Worst of all, I sometimes actually buy tabloids and read every creepy word.

It all started in 1986, when I spotted the headline: "Preacher Explodes During Sermon." I bought the paper for my father who's a minister.

Well, he did get a glimpse of it. But it became the first in my collection of "Baffling Spontaneous Combustion" stories.

The collection now includes a kissing couple who burst into flames—"Hundreds in shopping mall watch in horror. . ."—a woman whose hair exploded while she waited for a bus, and a rabbit that became a crispy critter for no reason.

I've even heard about an exploding bride, but I haven't found that story yet.

I'm a sucker for more than blowups. But, like the guy who only drinks Night Train Flambeau out of his paper bag, I'm choosy about my poison.

I don't care about the divorcing Mandrell sisters, Princess Di's latest cat spat, or gory details of Ted Bundy's execution. Give me a story about the jungle tribe of Elvis impersonators or leave me be.

Even though my first step in this downfall was a purchase for my dad, I can't really blame him. It was my grandfather who started the whole thing.

He was, after all, the one who had *Ripley's Big Book Believe It or Not!*

The book, we grandchildren were told, was not really bedtime reading. So my brother and I would wait until after bedtime, sneak downstairs and take scary peeks at its forbidden pleasures.

There was the man with horns growing out of his head, the people staring into the sun or buried alive for religious rites, the chicken that lived for seventeen days with no head.

Now *Ripley's Big Book* is mine, a family heirloom I treasure.

Still, I understand that along with the book I inherited a dangerous attraction to weird stories. I'm trying to overcome my addiction, trying to resist buying any more embarrassing tabloids.

Unless I find the exploding bride story.

Flying Fool

I'm not sure who first suggested I try flying a light plane. I only know it was not my idea.

I had never even set a trembling foot in a little plane, much less considered wrapping my white knuckles around its controls. But here I was, latest participant in the Aircraft Owners and Pilots Association's Fly a Friend program.

The program is a great idea. Members of AOPA take up people who might want to learn to fly.

They don't usually take up people whose first question about them is, "Can this guy handle somebody who panics? I mean, panics all over him?"

Assured that Chet Bowers—pilot since World War II and aerial photographer—could deal calmly with blowout hysteria, I arranged to take a spin in a Cessna 172.

9:45 a.m. We open up the hangar at the Nampa airport and guide the Cessna into the sunlight.

I'm shoving with all my might until Chet points out that the tiny plane is rolling by itself. The lead, it seems, is all in my feet.

9:50. We climb into the plane, me with my dashing white silk scarf tied around my neck and my heart in my throat.

I think I'm looking cool and calm. Then I ask Chet to show me exactly what I can grab on to. Somehow, he gets the message that I'm a little nervous. He patiently shows me an armrest on the door and says, "Or you can grab onto my arm if you want."

9:55. Chet goes through a list of items to be checked before takeoff. I refrain from voicing my own neurotic checklist on Chet, such as "Is there any history of insanity in your family?" We taxi to the runway.

10:00. Earplugs firmly in place, death grip on the seat and armrest, I prepare for takeoff.

10:02. Chet announces we're leveling off at 4,000 feet. I start wondering where the stewardess is with my drink.

10:03. We bank to the right. I'm on the down side. Chet informs me in a kind voice that I really don't have to lean into him every time he turns. I pray he doesn't notice that I've also had my eyes closed.

10:10. We're flying over Boise. Chet is pointing out the sights. Like a person recovering from a fever, I start getting interested in my surroundings.

10:15. We head up to Lucky Peak. It's a little bumpy, just like Chet said it would be. Somehow, the bouncing is fun.

10:30. We start back to the Nampa airport. A voice says, "Can I take over?" I can't believe this is me talking.

I grab the yoke, plant my feet firmly on the rudder pedals and try a two-inch bank to the right. I'm flying!

I venture a three-inch bank to the left. Chet assures me the plane won't pitch over and I go boldly for a five-inch bank.

10:45. Chet takes the controls for a perfect landing. We taxi in and he says, laughing, "Now get your white knuckles out of here."

I climb out, peel off my scarf and head into the pilot's lounge to swap flying stories.

Losing My Mind

I just ran across a most exciting study about older people and their minds.

According to all these scientists, whose names I can't remember right now, people's brains actually get sharper as they get older.

I wish I could tell you more about the study, but I've forgotten where I put it.

Anyway, I was really encouraged to hear that I'm brighter now, at forty-something, than I was at twenty. Not that I thought I was getting old or anything.

I know what old is. Old is my cousin Earl, who's ninety-five and makes no bones about it.

"I'm so old I don't even buy green bananas," Earl says.

No, old is not what troubles me. Getting there is the problem.

A while back, I noticed that I seemed to be losing people's names. Not people like my husband or my mother. Just actors like that woman who was in so many movies I like, only I can't tell you the names of any of them right now.

Then I started misplacing little things. Keys, pens, reminders I had written to myself for dates I had forgotten.

I began to realize these might be the real wonder years. I wonder who that friendly man was. I wonder where my glasses and my mind went. I wonder what I'm doing standing in the bathroom and how I got here.

The low point came a couple of weeks ago when I was talking to a friend and forgot the point of a story.

"Judy," my supposedly good friend said, "that's the second thing you've forgotten in the last five minutes."

"Really," I said, truly surprised. "What was the first?"

I started worrying. Was this the onset of aging?

I know in my heart that I'm not aging. That's for other people, not me or my friends. My friends, when I recognize them, tell me we're all doing just swell.

When we forget something, they say, it's just because we've lived such full lives. We've seen and done so much that our minds are filled to the brim with information.

That's why it takes us a while to remember what we're doing rummaging around in the front closet and who that person is in there with us.

In fact, a close friend, whose name escapes me at the moment, told me that another study has verified the overload theory. He, at least I think it was a he, said the study proved we take longer to make decisions because we have so many options to weigh.

A kid who only has life experience A or B can easily choose the right answer. We wise ones have to weigh endless possibilities.

I'm sure the studies are right. I'm sure our crackerjack minds are just getting better and better. I know by the time we're all ninety-five, we'll be as bright as Cousin What's-his-name.

Losing It Together

I'm not alone.

As I stumble along—losing my keys, my way and little bits of my mind—it's a comfort knowing others are out there in the dark with me.

Several weeks ago, I wrote a column about my slipping mind. In the first days after the column came out, I thought I was the only one forgetting names and the reason I walked into the kitchen.

Then, as people remembered they wanted to tell me something, I began to realize others are suffering, too.

"I liked your column on whatchamacallit," one friend said.

Another friend reassured me she was having similar problems.

"Sometimes I'm driving along and I can't remember where I'm going," she said.

If she finds no clues in her car—a birthday present, a small child who doesn't belong to her—she goes to the grocery store.

"I always need to go there," she said.

Robert Castle sent me solace in the form of a cartoon.

In the cartoon, a man sits in his pajamas on the side of a rumpled bed. He's staring fuzzily at a sign on his wall that says: "First pants, THEN your shoes."

Another friend called with the news that there's a new book out called "Old and Smart." I'm trying to remember to order it.

Carrol Valentine wrote a hilarious letter about young whippersnappers like me who think they know about aging.

As one ages, Valentine assured me, the skills for remembering are never lost. Oh, a few details may get lost in the shuffle, he admitted, but they're nothing compared to what one remembers.

"How do you tell 'kids' that such inconsequential details as forgetting what one had for breakfast hardly ranks up there with old Tom Edison and his invention of the cotton gin," he asked.

"Nobody said it would be easy coping with the aging process. But some seem to have more difficulty than one would expect, and the erudite Trudy McConnell may just be approaching a philosophical benchmark."

Very reassuring, Mr. Ballentine.

If I had any doubts left that memory loss has become a fad, a saleswoman in a card shop pointed out to me that there's now a card for people wandering around in a fog. Trust the card companies to spot a trend in the making.

Anyway, the card shows a fellow wearing a huge head bandage and saying, "Do I know me? That's why I carry Amnesia Express."

I like the idea of Amnesia Express. We all should have little cards we can pull out to check our names and addresses. Maybe we can even form a club. We can meet every other Wednesday night. Or any time that two of us remember to show up.

Selling the Baby

Feeling a little too comfortable in your home? Wishing your cozy nest could be visited and commented on by hordes of strangers?

Just plant a "For Sale" sign on your lawn and stand back.

A few months ago, thinking our lives were going way too smoothly, we decided to sell. We put up a sign. We thought we would be inconvenienced for a week or two.

After all, we'd heard the story about friends who sold their house while they were out buying Wheaties at Albertson's.

We'd read the headlines in the paper saying something like, "Everybody sells houses lickety-split."

We cleaned the place up. We threw away the piles of magazines, packed the college beer mugs and other decorating faux pas. We sat back smugly. The people showed up. They walked through. They didn't buy.

But they kept coming, through rain, sleet, and the dinner hour. And we kept hoping.

We heard how darling our place was. People loved the house, the yard, the decorating scheme, the location. They just didn't want to purchase any part of it.

Some of the visitors were Sunday drivers, just out for a stroll. But others were serious lookers.

Those were the people who usually showed up just as I was hauling the laundry past the front door to the washing machine.

The first guy to get the dirty laundry treatment was quite gracious. After pretending he didn't notice I was clutching a pair of underpants as I answered the door, he told me, "No problem. I'm a bachelor. I'm used to anything."

He did jump nimbly over the piles of dirty clothes, I noticed. But he didn't stay long and he didn't buy.

The other trick I used to bring potential buyers galloping to the front door was to get sick. Nothing like a good case of intestinal flu to make everyone want to see your house.

The first time it happened, I dragged out to the backyard and draped myself in a lawn chair.

Our excited would-be buyers got one glimpse of me and beat a quick retreat. I'm not sure, but I think they had handkerchiefs pressed to their faces.

The months wore on. The headlines continued to make announcements like: "Everyone in Boise sells homes except the Steeles."

We continued the daily ritual of making our house look as though no one lived there.

One day, I found myself loading wet laundry into the car to dry. Another day, I spent an hour in the garage looking in paper sacks for my toothbrush and the bills that needed immediate attention.

Just when it seemed nothing would ever happen, everyone decided to buy our house. We sold it to someone who promised to love it as much as we had. We signed on the line.

And then, after months of hoping for this moment, we cried.

Sports Shopping

My brother just told me he's been shopping for his wife.

"Mary's thinking about trying sea kayaking," he said. "I got her boots and slicker gear and a scarf with whales on it. She liked that best."

"Is she really going sea kayaking?" I asked.

"Maybe," he said.

Mary is the newest member of our family. But I already know I'm going to like her a lot. This woman is my kind of athlete. First the clothes, then the decision about trying the sport.

Don't get me wrong. Mary is an athlete. She and my brother got to know each other better by taking a month-long bike trek through Ireland.

If my husband and I had tried that early in our relationship, we wouldn't have had any later to our relationship.

But Mary obviously is an athlete who, like me, sees every sporting event as an opportunity for a cute new outfit.

I developed what I consider the correct sporting attitude early.

My friends were off skiing in their dungarees at age four. I didn't take any real interest in the sport until I found a great pink and green ski jacket with matching green stretch pants.

Once I got the ski outfit, I actually went skiing.

That hasn't always been the case. My father-in-law, detecting a slim interest in fly fishing, got me waders one year for Christmas. As I opened the box, visions of checked shirts with natty scarves began dancing in my head.

I haven't gotten out on the river once since then. But hey, I'm still searching for a smart-looking fishing vest and the perfect creel to add to the outfit. Then I might head out to some water.

Even I, fashion athlete that I am, didn't realize the athletic opportunities available in stores and catalogs until my brother mentioned the whale scarf.

I now find that every single sport you've ever even thought about has a special outfit.

Take snowshoeing. I consider snowshoeing more of a survival technique than a sport. You strap on the tennis rackets and trek out when the sled dogs die.

But now Sorel snowshoe boots come in tasteful pastel shades.

Hiking boots have been colorized, too. My good old brown leather boots let everyone know I've been hiking since God was young. These days, you have to wear something the color of your favorite Popsicle.

My hiking shorts aren't right either. I can wear them, but only if I wear my Lycra tights under them.

I have no Lycra tights. Somehow I started in-line skating without the required Lycra outfit. Now, I hear, there are Lycra skating shorts with hip and rear pads.

Even canoeing has special gear. You can buy paddling jackets, paddling gloves and, I'm not kidding, canoe jewelry.

I hope to buy a paddling outfit soon. Then I'll consider going canoeing. Maybe.

Goofing Off

Last week, my mother finally came clean.

It was an ordinary morning. We were sitting out on the back porch, having a cup of coffee.

Then she said, "I goofed off a lot when you kids were little."

I almost dropped my mug. This was my mother, who had just whipped up five dozen ginger cookies for us to freeze before breakfast.

That's the way she's always been, as far as I remember. Never frantic about getting things done, but always doing something. Certainly not "goofing off."

I asked her to explain.

"Oh, I'd be dusting and then I'd start thinking about something so I'd just sit down and think about it for a while," she said.

I always knew my mother spent time thinking. I just didn't know when she did it.

Obviously, she's been thinking recently that I need to learn about goofing off. She's right.

None of us spends enough time goofing off.

We're encouraged to make lists and check every item off. We're taught "duty first," "a stitch in time," "nose to the grindstone."

We're admonished to keep the competitive edge, feel the burn. Even if you do slip up and start goofing off, don't let it show. "Look busy."

We're so busy looking busy, we have no time left to think.

By goofing off, I don't mean wasting time. Wasting time is "looking busy."

Wasting time is sitting in front of the television with your mind on permanent hold.

Wasting time, as poet May Sarton says, is participating in mindless chatter at a party.

Goofing off, on the other hand, is talking with a good friend over coffee or dinner about your idea for saving the world. It doesn't even have to be practical. It just has to engage your brain.

Goofing off is digging in your garden whether you get every last tomato plant in the ground or not.

It is sitting in a chair on your back porch watching the squirrel circus in your trees. It is taking a walk without checking your heart rate.

Leisure activities are not always goofing off. They're often not even leisurely.

They usually have a goal, maybe even a team, a schedule and a score. They can be instructive. They can even be fun. But they're not goofing off.

Goofing off is throwing your dog a Frisbee. Goofing off is tossing a ball to your kid with no score, no rules, nothing but the ball slapping in your hand and your child learning to goof off.

Goofing off is letting your mind wander until it soars into uncharted air. Sometimes, it returns with nothing. Sometimes, it comes up with a creative new idea.

That's why problems often get solved at night.

The answers don't come when we're lying awake, grinding through all the obvious solutions. They come when we're asleep. The brain gets a chance to fly and finds a new solution.

Obviously, not every moment can be spent goofing off. The brilliant solution has to be put into action. The kids have to learn to do their chores. The books have to be dusted.

But somewhere in our daily lives, there should be a ten-minute gap that's unscheduled, unplanned. A short break set aside for "goofing off."

Remember: Mom knows best.

Family Pet

We have a new lawn.

It's green, it's pristine. It's beautiful. but, as far as some of my friends are concerned, it's lacking something.

They walk out my back door, survey the place and pronounce a death sentence on my lawn.

"What you need," they say, "is a dog."

I know they have my happiness at heart. I also have the sneaking suspicion that they can't stand a yard free of doggy deposits.

Listen to me, everyone. I do like dogs. Some dogs I love. Some day I may have a dog.

But I know too many people who were talked into friendly beasts and barely lived to tell about it.

Like my friend Arlene. Arlene's family had a sweet dog, Huckleberry, for thirteen years. When Huckleberry died, the family almost died too.

So it was not too hard for Arlene's son to convince her they needed Egbert. Like all kids' dogs, it ended up being Mom's charge.

And "charge" was the right word for Egbert. No matter how he was tied up, he managed to get out and run around.

The dogcatcher Judy got to know Egbert well.

The day he turned himself into the pound—just ran right up and scratched on the door—Arlene and Judy decided Egbert wasn't very bright.

The day not long after when he tried to evade Judy by jumping onto a full school bus, Judy told Arlene, "This dog is crazy. Get rid of him."

Eventually, Arlene did. Another unsuspecting soul, probably goaded by friends who thought her yard lacked the right amount of brown, saw Egbert in the pound. She fell in love with him.

Arlene packed up the dog's dish, leash, and food, and tried to look sad saying good-bye.

My friend Carolyn had a similar experience. Her beloved dog died and a friend spotted the perfect replacement.

Georgy looked gorgeous. No one would have suspected that she was literally a motor mouth.

After chewing her way through three sprinkler systems, she started working on the supports for Carolyn's second-story deck.

It finally got to the point that no one could step onto the deck. We were all afraid we'd bring it down on Georgy, busily gnawing below.

Carolyn was lucky. She found an innocent farm family to take her dog. But she still has nightmares that the dog is coming down the highway to find her.

Then there was the poor guy I met one night at a party. Someone in his family had dragged home a mutt for Dad.

Other dogs bring back trophies to lay at their masters' feet. This dog was eating the neighbors' garbage, then coming back to upchuck on his master's shoes.

Like the other hounds from hell, this dog eventually found another home. Probably with someone like me.

The Flu Fairy

All those who've had the flu, raise your hands.

I assume anyone whose hand is down is still too weak to lift a finger. No one I know has escaped that aching, coughing, wheezing, cramping in the belly feeling.

I thought I had.

I saw my husband go down like a felled redwood. I watched him suffering over dinner he couldn't taste, listened to him hacking in the lonely hours of the night.

I brought him aspirin, the heating pad, comfort. I, brave wife that I am, breathed the same air he did. I didn't even feel a twinge of flu.

Friends sagged around me. I stood strong.

Then I made the fatal mistake. I mentioned my good fortune. "Gee," I said, with just the smallest touch of smug. "I haven't gotten that ugly stuff. I must just live right."

The flu fairy heard me. She waved her germy little wand over me and I folded like the cream puff I really am.

I took to my bed. My husband started bringing me aspirin, hankies, comfort.

And somewhere in between watching the flu make tracks from my head to my innards and back again, I had a feverish insight.

Maybe being sick isn't that bad. You think you're miserable. You say you wish you could die. But all you have to do is lie there and try to keep breathing. It's those around you who are really suffering.

Like my poor hubby.

The first night, while I lay on the couch in my flattened state, he slaved away in the kitchen fixing me a nourishing meal. I decided my stomach wasn't up to it and rolled over.

The next night, he repeated the hot meal routine and added, "videotapes, honey!"

I opened one eye and tried to focus. Well, maybe I could watch a little of "Charade," one of my all-time favorites. He put it in our faithful VCR and discovered it didn't work. Not the tape, the blasted machine.

While I lay wrapped in my warm blankie, he ran back to the video store in the dead of night, dead of winter, and rented another VCR. I watched "Charade" with him sweating beside me, saying, "Isn't this fun?"

In the middle of the next night, I rolled over in my sleep and hacked directly into his ear.

He must have thought he was being wakened by something from "Exorcist." I drifted blissfully off again. He didn't sleep the rest of the night.

The next day was his birthday. I gave him a Swiss Army knife. He gave me a box of Fisherman's Friend Original Extra Strong Cough Drops. Then we canceled his big dinner out and he forked over another hot meal.

Now I'm feeling just a teeny bit better. I can sit up and take nourishment without any help. I probably could even get out of this bed if I wanted to.

But I'm not sure I want to. Now that I can focus again, I've been eyeing my husband. He's definitely looking puny, even listing a little.

Don't tell him I've noticed. He might crawl into bed and start enjoying himself again.

Homemade Havoc

I just found out I'm already behind on Christmas.

I'd cry if I weren't so relieved. Once again, I'm forced to drop all my crazy plans for homemade gifts.

I didn't realize that the holiday season was on us. I was still trying to get the lawn furniture put away when an article appeared in the paper with the warning: "Deadlines are coming up for sending packages through the U.S. Postal Service."

This was the year I was going to win the Christmas present Olympics. I actually started making gifts in June. I figured that way I wouldn't be down at the P.O. on Christmas Eve throwing large wads of cash at frazzled workers and screaming, "Carry it by hand if you have to . . . it's only going to New York."

I first tried to create a beautiful pin for my sister-in-law. Never mind that I've never made a piece of jewelry in my life. Never mind that I hate projects that involve teeny pieces of anything, especially beads and wire.

When that project bit the dust, I trudged hopefully on to the next hare-brained idea—a piece of art for my brother. Halfway through the cutting and gluing I realized I was going to have to use my expert watercolor techniques to bring the whole mess together.

I don't know any watercolor techniques. I don't have a clue about watercolors. It was, I thank the Lord, too late to sign up for a course. So that project ended up in the recycle bin.

Next, I decided to make shirts for all the guys. I blew the dust off my sewing machine—hey, so it's been a few years—and started waking up at 1 a.m. with sweaty nightmares about button holes.

My husband took pity on me and bought some really nice shirts for everybody.

This is not the first time I've been hit by the Christmas craft bug.

One Christmas dawn found me covered with paste and little bits of felt that were supposed to be glued to a banner for a friend. She lived in another state so she got the blasted thing some time in January. I told myself it made the present that much more special.

Another year, my mother opened up a box with half a bathrobe in it. To further dig myself in, I enclosed a note promising to finish the bathrobe so she wouldn't have to walk around with her stuffing hanging out.

The half-robe is still hanging in her closet, laughing at me when I visit her.

I've collected bottles to make fruit vinegars, pine cones and boughs for wreathes, cloth patches for skirts, purses and vests. None of them saw Christmas morning.

But hope, like a new crocus after the long winter, does spring eternal. I really, really believed that I would make wonderful gifts and be the toast of my family this year.

I haven't totally given up. I still have a few days left before the P.O. deadlines.

That should give me enough time to whip up a golf bag for my father-in-law, throw vases for all the women, take a wood-carving class. . .

Time Traveling

Have you ever noticed how life sometimes seems like a bad movie?

It happened to me last week. First, I went to my twenty-fifth college reunion, the only one I've attended. Then, in case I still hadn't noticed I was getting older, I had a birthday.

It was not even a big "O" birthday. But coming hard on the sight of college friends gone through a time warp, it could have done me in.

Friends and family gathered around in loving support.

One friend gave me a birthday card showing a woman screaming, "Oh my God!! I'm over the hill!" followed by the cheery message, "Yet another middle-aged person turns to religion."

My mother-in-law's card showed a ship laden with huge crates being lifted off by crane. The message: "Good Birthday News! Your candles are in."

I laughed myself silly over that card. After all, I'd already been through the painfully funny experiences that only a reunion can hand out.

There was the moment the class was given maps to the restaurant for dinner. Suddenly everyone was scrambling for glasses and magnifiers.

And there was the afternoon three of us who roomed together decided to visit our old digs.

We were trying to find our way through a maze of new fire doors when several helpful students showed up. Before long, they were peppering us with questions about college life "in the old days."

Finally one friend, whose bone-dry wit is still intact after all these years, turned to the kids questioning us and said, "Well, they got electricity the year after we graduated."

We aren't quite that old. But it did take me a while to adjust to the passage of twenty-five years across my friends' faces and lives.

Our homecoming queen is still a beauty with creamy skin and big dimples. She also has pure white hair.

My best friend, the one I took to college with me as protection against the unknown, has a son in college. I look at pictures of him and see the guys I was friends with in college. Now one of them has a grandchild.

Those of us who had gathered for this march into the past did spend a little time catching up on kids, parents, and jobs. We lingered for a bit on "remember the time" stories.

But most of our three days together was spent talking about ideas, hopes, and goals.

Nobody was worrying much about looks or wealth or fame. Many of my friends were searching for ways to make the world a better place.

We had serious discussions about life from the vantage point of seasoned travelers. We teased each other. We were comfortable together as only people can be who've known each other as young and goofy kids.

I discovered again that true friends are friends forever.

We had taken different roads to get to this gathering. But we had arrived at many of the same reasons for living.

The reunion probably wasn't the stuff of a great movie. But it was a great way to start the second half of my life.

Rites of Spring

Spring is definitely here. Kites are braving the winds. Kids are skating past my front door wearing shorts. And something is growling in my basement.

No, it's not a hibernating bear. It's everything I did and didn't do last winter. And last fall. It's all waiting to be cleaned up, put away, fixed, sorted, thrown out.

There are other monsters lurking in my closets. My garage is a horror show.

It is, as sure as robins hopping on the lawn, time to do some spring cleaning. Or rather, time to feel guilty about not doing it.

None of this mattered in the winter. It was too snowy to worry about anything except building a big fire and stretching out with a book. Too cold to do more than shove the mess under the bed with a muttered vow to "get at this when the weather's better."

Now the weather is gloriously better. And I'm stuck, once again, in one of the loveliest seasons of the year, trying to imagine what there is in our DNA that links "spring" with cleaning.

Don't misunderstand. If you come to my house, you won't be nauseated. Surfaces will be showing. The house will look straightened up.

That's because you're polite. Your mother taught you never to snoop in people's drawers. If she didn't tell you to stay out of people's basements, I will convince you at knife point.

My mother taught me to be polite and to be neat.

"Put everything away," she said. Her second rule, "and once in a while, haul it all to the dump," I somehow missed.

This winter, I did make a stab at it. Honest, Mom. I went through one closet and sorted out clothes to give away. The pile sat on a chair upstairs for a month. Then, it was shoved back into its closet when friends came over for dinner.

Finally, in another cleaning frenzy, I dragged the pile to a chair by the back door. It's still sitting there, near the paperwhite bulbs I was going to force and the ski boot bag that goes back in the basement.

Maybe I'm being too hard on myself. Maybe points should be given for any effort made. I mean, I did get the lawn furniture and the hammock put away before the snows came.

And I shoveled out a tower of old magazines threatening to kill me in my little bed. Of course, another four stacks have sprung up. But that doesn't count because they're all dated after 1989.

The ski boot bag now has my ski boots sitting right beside it. They haven't made it into the bag, much less down to the basement. But, hey, I tried.

The Christmas wreaths are down. My husband actually removed them and put them in garbage bags. But I see no difference between doing my own chores and nagging someone else to do them.

The Christmas ornaments actually made it into the basement. I'm sure I'll get them back into their proper shelves any day now.

Unless I come across my hammock first.

A Moving Experience

I love watching the little birdies come home.

I see them moving into their nests and think, "Thank the blessed stars it's not me."

Summer is moving time. According to a recent newspaper article, fifty million people will move this year. One-third of them will move in June, July and August.

That's about seventeen million people hurtling down America's highways with all or pieces of everything they own.

They will be crazed from the brain-numbing exercise of packing or tossing every single object in their houses. They will be dizzy from lack of sleep and the nagging worry that the savings bonds and Grandma's jewels went into the Salvation Army box.

They will be roadway menaces. I know because I've driven down that highway before. I was not a pretty sight.

Being a minister's daughter gave me a taste for the open road. Each move we made was memorable in its own awful way.

The one I liked best was the year Daddy and I went to church camp and Mom and my brother had to do most of the moving.

Nowadays, my father and I could whine about not having closure on one phase of our lives. Back then, we were just grateful the moving members of the family had made any space at all in the new house for our stuff.

But the move my parents will never forget sounds like something from "The Grapes of Wrath."

Heading out of Chicago in a pickup filled with everything from books to the washing machine and topped by a mattress, they made it most of the way to Kansas City before the rains set in.

They dragged every soggy item but the washing machine into a motel room. They then spent a happy summer night alternately turning on the heat to dry their goods and running the air conditioning to keep themselves from frying.

The next morning, fellow motelers were startled to see a bedraggled couple muscling a mattress out of their room and throwing it on top of their crammed truck. It's a wonder they weren't arrested.

Being a slow learner, I moved a lot after I left home. For some reason I still don't understand, the worst moves were the shortest distance—from one part of Boise to another.

Start off saying, "It's just around the corner, really," and you can bet you'll end up some midnight heaving drawers full of clothes into a car filled with house plants and the dog.

Moving is like childbirth, though. No matter how many times you do it, you forget how agonizing it is.

Our last move, I knew that this time I was organized. Boxes were carefully labeled, lists kept. The movers assured us it would take no more than a morning to get us the few blocks to our new house.

Some time in the night, they finally left us. As I collapsed into a bed surrounded by mounds of clothes, kitchen gear, and boxes that had defiantly shed their labels, I swear I heard a birdie laughing at me.

Instruction Madness

The instruction police are running amuck.

In the old days, they confined their lists of instructions to heavy machinery, swing-set kits, and cans of ready-to-bake biscuits. Now they're everywhere.

I hate instructions. It used to be I could avoid them.

I never bought anything stamped "Easy to Assemble." I left all items with cords to my husband. I made Campbell's Soup and Jello any old way I pleased.

But lately, manufacturers have gone berserk with instructions. Viewing the buying public with a skeptical eye, they've decided to leave nothing to chance. Everything these days is wrapped in a long and detailed lists of do's and don't's.

I bought a razor a little while ago. It came, of course, in several layers of plastic.

There were no instructions on exactly which tools and teeth to use to get the blasted thing undone. But when I finally wrestled the package open, its contents included a three-page pamphlet called "How to Shave Your Legs."

The family gave my mother-in-law a radio/cassette player for Christmas. Not seeing the look of fear in my eyes, she asked me to help her with the operating instructions.

There were several pages of rules on connecting the flotsam to the jetsam. Right in the middle was the one instruction I understood: "Don't sit on the cord."

A little while ago, I had an ironing board cabinet installed in a wall. The cabinet came with an official-looking brochure on operating procedure for the board. My favorite instruction was the one no kid who's been dinged by a flying board would ever forget: "Close door securely."

There was more. My board also came with a list of ironing tips, such as "Iron early in the day when you're not tired" and "Learn to iron with unhurried, well-directed rhythmic motions, never quick or jerky strokes."

Right. It's morning. You're pooped, despite the instruction police's assumption that you're fresh early in the day. You've got five seconds to get your shirt ironed and yourself out the door and you're worrying about your jerky strokes.

But the worst list—the one suggesting that the manufacturers have finally cracked—came with a pair of beaded shoes.

I'm not kidding. I thought I knew how to handle a pair of shoes, but I was wrong. There are shoe laws and the instruction police will enforce them.

"These shoes were designed to wear in the daytime, to go to the supermarket, watch soap operas and/or baby walking," my shoe procedure list states. "They are delicate and should not be worn to play baseball, football, or hockey."

Thank goodness they told me. I was about to slip them on for a little backyard scrimmage. If I can locate a baby to walk, I might avoid arrest.

Planning for Change

In my younger days, I used to plan.

I wrote down appointments in a datebook, carefully noted on my wall calendar every scheduled night out. Then, all innocence, I expected every one of them to happen.

When they didn't, I got cross. And eventually, disillusioned.

I entered what I called my Blue Period. Why bother to plan, I asked myself. Nothing's going to work out anyway. Then I talked to my cousin Linda. Younger but wiser than I, Linda set me straight.

"You plan," she said with a laugh, "so you'll know when your plans have fallen through."

Linda knows about plans coming apart. She has little children. Kids can disassemble a master plan faster than a salesman on TV can slice and dice a cucumber.

You're looking forward to a night on the town. You're bathed, you're dressed, you have money to burn and a friend to play with. Then your child wanders in, glassy-eyed and hot, and throws up on your loafers. You say bye-bye to your plans, to say nothing of your shoes.

But little kids aren't the only schedule breakers. In these shaky times, anything can happen to your perfect plans.

Like that forty-ton space station that's supposed to fall on our heads any day now.

The experts, who I imagine to be a little knot of men huddled in a shelter, said that it was "impossible to predict where debris might land."

To soften the blow, so to speak, they said that the station was "unlikely to be a hazard to people or property."

Right. The equivalent of an ocean liner may suddenly make a dive for my head, but I'm supposed to carry on with my dinner plans as if nothing is happening.

If that doesn't make you hesitate with the dinner reservations, try the threat of a breaking dam.

The folks over in Hermiston, Oregon, were told recently that their eighty-three-year-old dam is a "high-risk structure." If they're doing any planning at all, it's probably to test the chicken coop for float potential.

It doesn't take a skydiving station or crumbling dam to ruin a well-laid plan. Sometimes even good news can mess up your perfect strategy.

The Soviet KGB assigned to East Germany learned that fact.

They thought they had a good deal sewed up for life. Then peace broke out and pulled the wall down around their ears. There are still 10,000 of them casting around Germany for something to do.

It's hard to land a job when your resume reads: "Agent with high-collar trench coat seeks dangerous work in the cold. Adept at skulking and taking pictures with fountain pens. Don't call; I'll find you."

They need to talk to my cousin Linda. She'll get their plans and their priorities in order.

Good Old Days

I've always wondered about those guys advertising books on ways to get rich.

Why are they out hawking books instead of getting rich themselves?

Now I know the answer. For I too have a great money-making scheme. But, like them, I want someone else to do it.

So, for anyone out there who'd like to soar higher than King Midas and be considered a prince in the process, here's my idea: Go back to the good old days.

I'm not talking trying to turn back the clock. I'm talking remaking the clock, especially that giant alarm clock with the little bells on the top.

That clock was straightforward. It had a big face with big hands that said, "Here's the time." Its no-nonsense bell left no doubt that you'd better get out of bed, bub.

There were no silly digital numbers, no frou-frou buttons to let you fudge on your wake-up call. You got right up and you started your day.

You were ready to get up with that clock. You hadn't spent the whole night tortured by lit-up numbers and blinking dots.

I need that alarm clock. I'll pay good money for that alarm clock. And for a lot of other great things that have disappeared in the last few years.

I'd like to own a solid black phone with a dial.

So what if it took a few more seconds to place a call. You knew you'd gotten somewhere when you were through dialing those seven numbers. Or rather, those five numbers preceded by a word.

Yes, kids, phone numbers used to start with a word. My first phone number began with "Pearl 3." The second started off "Spruce 7."

Those phone numbers conjured up images of ocean and forest. Those phone numbers, civilized and easy to remember, were as solid as the heavy phones that went with them.

Speaking of heavy equipment, here's to the good old bikes we all pedaled to school. They had fat, comforting tires, a basket big enough to really hold stuff and a bell to ring. The handlebars and seats put you upright like a real human being instead of hunched over like a giant frog.

These bikes, in a modified form, are coming back. They're called mountain bikes and they're expensive. Someone, folks, is making money off of them.

A few other good old things have reappeared.

I just spotted a new old-fashioned radio with an on-off button that makes a satisfying click and a dial for changing stations. The only thing it doesn't have is "Amos and Andy," "Suspense," or "Big John and Sparky."

And smart people have started making classic toys, such as Erector Sets, Flexible Flyer Sleds, and Raggedy Ann and Andy dolls. These are not cheap toys. In one catalog, the Erector Set is $48.50, the sled is $52 and the dolls $43.50 each.

At those prices, a person could get rich. Quick.

Back to School

The heat may be with us, the days long and blazing. But when August starts heading toward September, I get ready to go back to school.

It's been twenty years since I actually picked up my books and headed off to class. But every fall I start preparing mentally for the first day of school.

It's something you never outgrow, the nervous excitement that September brings.

My husband talks about being "ready for school" when he's going to work. My brother and I talk about taking classes at our local colleges. My mother buys "back-to-school" supplies for her office.

When I was little, the back-to-school ritual always began by buying supplies.

My brother, mother, and I would start at Hested's Five and Dime where we picked out Big Chief tablets, extra-fat pencils, Pink Pearl erasers, and a Hopalong Cassidy pencil box with a red ruler for a lid.

Then we'd go to Couch's shoe store for a new pair of shoes and to May D&F for my new dress and my brother's pair of long pants.

The clothes were special, even before I started picking them out myself. The new supplies were pored over at home like our Halloween loot.

But it wasn't just having new things that made the buying ritual exciting.

It was the idea of a fresh beginning, another chance at the happy life you thought you were going to have last year in school.

This year, you were going to get a great teacher who never marked any of your answers wrong or gave tests when you weren't ready. She was going to find you brilliant.

You were going to be in a class with all your best friends, who were going to love you unconditionally. You were going to discover a cure for cancer and look cool doing it.

The new year always turned out just like the rest of life—some joys, some sorrows, some days when you thought the bell would never ring.

But I always had hopes, as I bought my Big Chief tablet and my forty-eight-Crayola box, that this year would be different.

In two weeks, one of my best friends is starting kindergarten. He has a list of supplies he needs. Just looking at it brings back good memories.

There are no Big Chief tablets. Some of the crayon colors have been changed. And paste, which used to be a basic element of every activity from papier-mache to lunch, has been taken off the list.

But he and his brother and sister are out buying my youth—folders with pockets, three-ring binders with thick stacks of ruled paper, blunt-end scissors, pencils, rulers and Pink Pearl erasers.

They're waiting with fluttery stomachs to find out which teachers they have and which friends are their classmates. They're hoping, like we did, that this year will be perfect.

I'm beyond all that now. I know my year probably won't be perfect. Unless, of course, I get the right teacher and the right notebook.

ON A SERIOUS NOTE

Inflaming the Discussion

The recent torching of the Women's Health Care Clinic put more to flames than a building. It also scorched the idea that Boise is a place where people with differing ideas can have an honest, calm disagreement.

No one has been arrested for the fire. No one knows for sure that abortion was the reason for the arsonist's flames.

But abortions were performed at the clinic. The clinic was the site of protests by anti-abortion groups in the past. It's safe to assume, and groups on both sides of the abortion issue are assuming, that abortions brought out the arsonist and the match.

Whatever the warped reasons, the arsonist harmed us all.

The clinic's patients and staff are obviously affected the most. Women came there to get abortions, which is their legal right. They also came for other health services including pregnancy tests.

Now they, and the staff who served them, must meet in other quarters until the clinic is rebuilt. They must deal with the confusion of new routines in new places and medical records that have been damaged.

The clinic's staff was not frightened by the fire. They stated their determination to continue serving their patients and to rebuild the clinic.

Still, there is no question that this kind of violence leaves its mark on everyone involved with the clinic.

It also leaves an ugly mark on the groups opposing abortion. Some people opposing abortion understand that.

Several years ago, I wrote a pro-choice column. After it came out, I received more than one hundred letters and phone calls. Most of the people responding agreed with me. Several of the letters and phone calls, as I had expected, were filled with hate. But, among the responses were three thoughtful letters from people who disagreed with me and wanted to tell me why.

The letters were emotional, but courteous. They didn't change my mind. But they did make me think long and hard about the opposition to legalized abortion. And they made me realize, as the clinic fire so graphically demonstrated, that neither side wins with violence.

One of the letters addressed violence directly.

"I oppose abortion," the writer said. "But I also oppose the violence that some pro-life groups are promoting. Where is the group for me? Where is my voice?"

After the clinic fire, members of several anti-abortion groups denounced the torching. They understood that the violence harms their cause. It drives apart opposing sides, leaving no room for discussion or understanding.

The fire may have been set in the name of those opposing abortion. But, by torching the clinic, the arsonist has inflamed more than the question of abortion. The arsonist has managed—by force, by fear, and fire—to burn all of us. No matter what our beliefs.

Family Values

I'm sick of hearing about family values.

Please understand. I believe strongly in the values my family taught me.

But those values have almost nothing in common with the buzz phrase "family values" that's being tossed out carelessly by so-called pro-family political candidates, preachers, and members of some right-wing groups.

These people are taking the word "family" and twisting it to their own ends.

I have to admit they confused me for a while.

I like the idea of family. I like my family and some other people's families, too. And I believe that we and our children need strong values that are passed on by parents, grandparents, aunts and uncles, even siblings.

So why do I squirm every time the "F" phrase is thrown at us in harangues from public figures?

Because the public figures beating us over the head with "family" have a narrow definition of what is a true American family.

Anyone who deviates from the Beaver Cleaver image of family is looked at with suspicion, or ignored, or dismissed as undesirable by these people.

I was raised in a Beaver Cleaver family—two parents, two kids. Dad went to work. Mom stayed home, at least while I was little. We even had a house with a white picket fence.

I also was raised, as I believe and hope many of us were, to understand that the world is full of different kinds of people. Not threatening, just different.

By example, and by word, I grew up learning that tolerance is part of being a family member and one of my family's strongest values.

Which is not to say my parents were lackadaisical about our way of living.

We had definite rules. We went to church together. We ate breakfast and dinner together. We solved arguments by talking, not fighting. We had chores and were expected to do them.

But other families weren't expected to live by our rules. In one of my friends' families, Sunday was for lounging around. In another, Dad made breakfast and nobody cleaned house.

Eventually, I learned that people could be different from us in other ways and still be a family.

They could be a different color or speak a different language, go to a different church or no church at all. They could be divorced or single with children. They could have a mother who worked and a father who stayed home. They could be gay or lesbian.

They could be poor, on welfare, old or ill and that didn't make them any less of a family.

And they could be part of my family whether I was related to them or not.

At one time or another, my family has included a neighbor I called Grandma and two women I thought of as second mothers.

Now it includes my in-laws, the family of my godchild and other friends who accept me even when I do something they don't like.

That's what a family is.

Not the Cleavers with their perfect children and their impossibly perfect lives, but real people who are tolerant of each other and love each other no matter what.

To be truly pro-family means to accept and support families in all their amazing variety.

Instant War

The following column was written during the Gulf War.

This week, we fought a minute-to-minute war.

As I write this column, wailing sirens are sending Israelis into gas masks and a chill through the newsroom. It's the latest assault warning in the Iraqi war and the most recent assault on our nerves.

For the first time in history, those of us at home have been bombarded with the sights and sounds of war at the same time they are happening. We've gone on a roller coaster ride of emotions, experiencing moments of intense reality and moments that seem completely unreal.

We knew the exact minute the missiles began finding their targets in Baghdad. We listened—fastened almost helplessly to our television sets—as the bombs exploded and reporters edged back to windows to give us the direction of the blasts and describe the fires that followed.

And then, an incredibly short two hours later, we heard analysis on the mission from the president, other politicians, and the military. It had all happened too fast to seem real.

During that short night, we went from despair that war was actually upon us, to fear for our pilots and the innocent people receiving their hail of bombs, to elation that it all seemed to be over.

The elation was short-lived.

The next day, we woke to the nightmare possibility that more destruction was coming.

That evening, a televised discussion by Middle East experts was interrupted with the sickening news that Israel was being hit by missiles. We saw, for the first time, the eerie picture of reporters talking through gas masks.

We stayed in front of our televisions, where we were unnervingly warm and safe, watching surreal images of a world coming apart.

We saw bombs flying into doorways of buildings in Iraq and blowing out the four walls of the Iraqi air force headquarters. We were given visions of a disconcertingly beautiful hell as the nighttime sky over Baghdad glittered with the fire of incoming missiles.

We heard military analyst Anthony Cordesman's chilling description of the Iraqi people's life this week: "They must stay inside, hidden. They never know when something will be coming over the horizon. It will hit them before they know they're under attack."

And we saw the heartbreaking grin of Michael Scott Speicher, the first American casualty, in a Christmas video sent home to his family.

When Tom Brokaw, reporting on missile attacks in Israel, learned that only conventional missiles had been fired, he said, "It's hard to believe I'm saying this, but things look brighter because we only have a conventional missile attack on Tel Aviv. This is the world we live in."

He's right. The war has become our world. It's with us every minute now, updated almost second by second. And we stand by, filled with conflicting hope and dread, and watch the beast rage.

A Plea for Peace

The following column was written during the Gulf War.

I'm not naive.

Whenever I talk about the need to fight for peace, people find my plea naive.

I admit that it can sound naive to believe that peace has a chance in the midst of war. But I believe strongly that we move in the direction we're preparing to move.

If we're preparing for war with weapons and troops, we'll likely have war. If we're planning for peace, peace has a chance.

Perhaps my plea for peace sounds naive because it lacks cynicism.

Cynicism can be a cop-out, an easy way to avoid having to work for an idea. If we believe that nothing we do affects the world, we can sit back in our misery and watch events happen to us.

But the growing cynicism in our country, and it is growing, comes not from a desire to let everything slide. It comes from a deep feeling of helplessness.

So much in the United States is going wrong.

The economy is shaky. Our debt is mounting, our banks are closing. Layoffs are being reported daily. We're worried about big companies folding, other countries buying our best resources and minds.

Our air is dirty, our water is foul. The homeless are trapped and starving in the streets of this land of plenty. Violence shreds our cities. Drugs are overtaking our children and possibly our future.

And now we are at war, for reasons we cannot fully understand.

We know our country has lost some of its bright promise. We know much of what is happening is wrong. But we feel helpless to make a difference.

So we sit quietly and pray that our leaders know what they are doing, know more than we do. Or we become cynical, hardened to the hope that anything will get better.

Nothing will get better if we don't make it happen. We're the only ones who can make a difference.

If it takes being naive to get us out of our chairs and into the streets, then I will stand on the side of naivete.

Not all of us can literally go into the streets. Some of us don't think protesting in the streets does any good. Some of us think it is effective but can't bring ourselves to march.

But there are other ways to add your voice to the cry for peace.

Write a letter to a representative in Congress who stood up for peace. Sign a petition. Work for a politician you believe in. Make a peace quilt. Find your talent and use it for peace.

We do have the power—to inform our friends and fellow citizens, to elect, to question our leaders' motives, to demand accountability from the people in office and those running for office.

We can make our voices heard. But we won't if we cynically, perhaps even naively, decide to keep quiet.

Standing Up to Harassment

It happened out of the blue.

I was called into the boss's office to talk about "work problems." But the conversation veered off into talk about the way I looked and dressed.

I left feeling confused and angry. I said nothing about it, afraid I had somehow brought the incident on myself.

Only after the man had moved on to another company did I hear similar stories from other women in my office.

My response to sexual harassment was not helpful, but it was typical.

An Idaho Human Rights Commission pamphlet on sexual harassment states that victims don't speak up because they "feel ashamed of what has happened to them. They are afraid that other people will say they 'asked for it,' that no one will believe them, that they won't be able to prove their allegations, or that they will be branded as troublemakers."

Despite the fears and threats, more people in Idaho are standing up to their harassers, according to the Idaho Human Rights Commission director Marilyn Shuler.

Shuler says thirty-one cases alleging sexual harassment were filed during the commission's last fiscal year.

In the first four months of this fiscal year, the commission has already seen thirty-two cases filed. More are in the system.

But others are still the victims of unwanted sexual conduct at work. They don't know that they may be able to end their suffering.

Victims need first of all to recognize that they are being victimized, often by someone in a position of power.

In a random sampling of commission cases from the last two years, Shuler found that eighty-eight percent of the harassers were company owners, managers, or supervisors over the victims.

"It has almost nothing to do with sex," she says. "It is an act of power."

Victims have to arm themselves with information. Federal and state laws are on their side. Many companies have anti-sexual harassment policies as well.

And Shuler and others at the commission can give them information on ways to stop sexual harassment and where to go for help.

Victims have to find the initial courage to speak up. But they don't have to do it alone.

The rest of us must recognize that sexual harassment is a real and damaging problem. We need to support our fellow workers when the problem exists. We need to listen seriously to our employees' allegations of possible harassment.

I hope that I'm never the victim of sexual harassment again. I hope that no one I work with goes through the pain of harassment.

But, if it does happen to me or a colleague, I need the courage to speak out. Otherwise, the ugly secret will continue to fester.

Hate and Fear

Hi! I'm from the hate state.

Idaho hasn't taken up that slogan yet. But we could be hit with it if we decide to pass the anti-gay initiative.

We'll deserve it.

The initiative is rooted in hate and fear of differences. In other states, where similar initiatives have been considered, the hatred that has surfaced has been disturbing. And it has stirred up more hatred.

Hate crimes doubled last year in Portland, Oregon, when an anti-gay amendment was considered, according to Captain Dan Noelle of the Portland Police Department.

Barbara Perrin, a friend of my family's, lives in Eugene. She saw firsthand what can happen when a campaign against one group of people starts.

"One word describes the whole movement—divisive," she says.

Perrin, a mother of two, was very aware of the effect the debate had on her children, particularly her nine-year-old son.

"It created a lot of unease, where I don't think any unease would have been felt otherwise," she says. "They sensed anger and strong emotions on both sides. They got the feeling that it could affect them, but they didn't know how."

The questions and anxiety raised in children's minds made Barbara and many other parents angry.

"There were a lot of letters to the editor from parents saying, 'My kids are coming home asking me questions they wouldn't have under ordinary circumstances.'"

Oregon's amendment failed and hate crimes decreased.

But in Colorado, where a similar amendment passed, the number of crimes against homosexuals increased and is still up.

So is membership in groups fighting the anti-gay measure.

Don Bossart, a family friend who teaches in Denver, is a member of the Parents and Friends of Lesbians and Gays. The group was one of many that rallied against Colorado's anti-gay amendment.

"We worked hard and thought we had the amendment defeated," Bossart says.

When it passed, everyone who had fought it was shocked.

"We were very disappointed and depressed. But then a strengthening began to occur," he says.

"People have galvanized around the loss . . . . More people are joining our group because they were infuriated at the loss of freedom. We will make a change."

Their determination is admirable. It's easy to wish, as Brian Bergquist says some people are hoping, "that this will all go away and the sun will come up tomorrow."

But Bergquist, chairman of Idaho for Human Dignity which opposes the anti-gay initiative in Idaho, knows the anti-gay movement won't disappear.

The rest of us need to face reality as well.

The initiative is not going away. It will continue to raise fear and anger. We will have to face the fears head on, be willing to talk to people about the motives behind the initiative.

If we don't, we could become the hate state.

Growing Pains

The news is disturbing but not surprising.

As Boise grows, its violence is growing. The latest example is fights between drivers.

In recent weeks, several drivers have assaulted other drivers or their cars. One driver allegedly tried to stab a seventeen-year-old in the throat. Another chased a pizza delivery person with a hammer. A third attacked a car with a shovel.

We're a city with growing pains, a small city used to wide streets with little traffic, unlocked doors, stores with no lines, and smiling sales clerks who know your name.

Now it's all changing faster than we can keep up. And it's sad to see it happening.

I didn't grow up in Boise, but I grew up in a place like Boise.

When I was a small child in Denver, my brother and I walked to the candy store armed only with pennies and a reminder from our mother to "look both ways."

As teenagers, we took the bus downtown on Saturdays and spent the day at the main library or art museum, in the department stores, or at the movies.

By that time, Denver was growing and so were its problems. We stayed away from Larimer Street, where the "winos" hung out, and the Five Points area where there might be street fights.

But it wasn't until I arrived in Chicago a few years later that I learned big city survival rules: Don't look at anyone in the street. Keep the doors to your house and car locked, even when you're there. Stay alert at all times. Suspect every stranger.

The one time I left my car door unlocked, somebody rifled through my car while I was walking a friend to her door.

I did, thank heavens, have the back door to my apartment locked the day I saw a man's face staring at me through the door's window.

"Don't scream," he said.

I screamed as loud as I could and ran out into the front hall.

When I went back into my kitchen, armed with neighbors who came running at my screams, the man was gone.

That's the point of the story. Not that the face in the window disappeared, but that the neighbors didn't. Even in a big city, there were communities of people who cared about each other.

The whole city of Boise is still like my apartment building in Chicago. I have no doubt that if I screamed here, people would run to my rescue. I know that when I smile at people on the street, they'll smile back.

We have to preserve that feeling of community. It's not just nice, it's necessary for the survival of our city.

Those of us who live here and know what life in Boise has been have to maintain a balancing act as our city grows. We must learn to protect ourselves in a changing town. But we have to juggle that defensive posture with the friendliness and concern for others that make Boise the city we love.

The alternative—watching our community turn in on itself out of fear—is no choice at all.

Learning to Die

I now know how to kill myself.

The fellow who sold me *Final Exit*, my instruction book for suicide, said: "You're one of the lucky ones."

He meant I was one of the people on a waiting list who actually received the book.

Many people in Boise are still waiting for their copies of *Final Exit*. Employees at local bookstores are taking names and hoping the copies will show up soon.

The little book with the clinical white cover has become an unexpected best seller.

Final Exit is by Derek Humphry, founder of the right-to-die Hemlock Society. The book gives specific information for committing suicide. It also says that while suicide is not a crime, helping another person to die is unlawful.

And it states that it was written for the mature adult suffering an unbearable terminal illness.

More than 200,000 copies have been sold and more are being ordered. Some people might be buying *Final Exit* out of curiosity or morbid interest. I have to admit when I first read a review of the book I was only curious about it, nothing more.

But, by the time my copy actually arrived, I'd begun to feel strangely comforted that it would be on my book shelf.

I have no desire to kill myself, no wish to put my family and close friends through my suicide. I also don't want to put myself or them through an agonizingly long and painful last illness.

Many of us have seen friends or relatives suffer a terrible death.

Many of us have wondered if it wouldn't be better to take out the tubes, stop the tests and surgery and let our beloved friend die in peace.

At some point, we've also had to wonder what our own end will be like.

We're blessed with medical care and cures that give us longer and healthier lives. But with the cures comes the possible curse that we will linger painfully with no hope of recovery. Our doctors may still be handcuffed by laws saying they cannot help us or allow us to die.

The last time I saw my grandmother alive, she was full of life. She was chasing one of her great-grandchildren around the living room. The little boy was shrieking happily. She was laughing.

Shortly after, she suffered the first of many strokes. Her life slowly chipped away until there was no joy left. She said she was ready to die.

When she began hemorrhaging, the doctors prepared for surgery. The family said, "No more," and my grandmother died peacefully. She was ninety-five.

I hope to live a healthy life like my grandmother did for many years. I hope when I'm dying, others will be allowed to help me leave.

Until that time, I'll keep my copy of *Final Exit*.

Thanksgiving

They were often cold, wet, hungry. They fought disease, fires, wolves, and terrors of the unknown.

The Pilgrims lived lives most of us can't even imagine today. But, in some ways, we may not be better off than they were.

Don't misunderstand. I wouldn't want to face the Pilgrims' first year. But the problems we've created since then make life equally difficult.

When the Mayflower sailed on September 6, 1620, she had 102 passengers and around 20 crew members. Only one of the passengers died on the voyage.

But during the first year, thirteen of eighteen wives, nineteen of twenty-nine single men, and half the crew died.

By that first Thanksgiving, the group had been cut in half by death. Several families were completely gone.

At the same time, the Pilgrims were settling into a land so abundant that they thought it was a wilderness.

They had deer, ducks in the hundreds of thousands, partridge, and wild turkeys.

The Indians had shown them how to fish. They had striped bass, cod, lobster, eels. The shores were thick with clams and oysters. The woods were full of berries.

They could drink water out of the rivers. The air was pure. And so was their resolve to stay together in their new land, whatever the costs.

When the Mayflower returned to England after that dreadful first winter, not one Pilgrim decided to go back.

Today, most of us live well compared to the Pilgrims. When we are cold, we turn on the heat. When we need food, we go to the store. When we are ill, we see a doctor.

But we've paid a price for our comfort. Our water and air are polluted. Our wild animals are dwindling. Many of us who are sick or poor are ignored or forgotten.

We live with the threats of nuclear war, AIDS, toxins in our food, a collapse in the economy. And our biggest threat may be our own dwindling resolve to save ourselves.

The Pilgrims banded together, supported each other in the face of death. We look at our polluted land, our homeless, our corrupt politicians, and we retreat.

We still have much to be thankful for. As we count our blessings, we can also ask for resolve to stand together against the terrors we've created and allowed.

With courage, we can win back a piece of the paradise the Pilgrims found.

Facing the End

For a few days, the world stared into the nuclear abyss.

That was thirty years ago. But those of us who lived through the Cuban missile crisis in October, 1962, will not forget it.

Now that secret documents from the crisis are being opened, experts are expressing surprise and dismay at how close we and the Russians came to bombing each other into oblivion.

The analysts knew then that the situation was serious but assumed it was handled smoothly. Now—as they read about day-long delays of communications between Nikita Khrushchev and President John Kennedy and about messages delivered by bicycle—they know better.

But all of us listening to the news reports those few days in October had no doubt that the world could end at any moment.

At one point, the father of a boy I was dating called to ask my father if I could leave town with their family. They were going to their mountain cabin where they felt they would be safe from nuclear attack. They wanted to take me with them.

My father said no, that I would stay home. I was relieved. I didn't know then that going to the mountains wouldn't have saved us. I only knew I wanted to be with my family, even if it meant dying together.

The last day of the crisis, my brother and I stayed home from school. That was unusual. My father stayed home from work. That was very unusual.

I remember us sitting in the breakfast nook. We pulled the television in from the den and listened to reports on TV and on the radio. We sat together, we ate together. We talked about what was happening, even reminisced about our family.

Looking back, it could have been an average Saturday at my house. But hanging over everything was the black possibility that we would have to watch the world incinerate itself.

I remember asking my dad what we would do if we heard the awful announcement that the bombing had started.

"We'll go into the back yard," he said, "and watch it come."

He wasn't being flip, wasn't making fun of my fear. He was being reasonable in an insane situation. You have one choice. You huddle inside or you go out and face it head on.

He and my mother were calm. They, like everyone else in their generation, had faced dying young during World War II.

But for my brother and me, it was our first glimpse of death. The bogeyman was very real and shaped like a mushroom cloud.

The crisis ended. Khrushchev agreed to Kennedy's demands that the Soviet Union take their missiles out of Cuba. Kennedy pledged not to attack the island.

Our world righted itself. My brother and I went back to school. Our parents went back to work. I started worrying again about grades and dates.

But my world was a darker place. I knew, as I never had before, that it could end without any warning at all.

Mountain Thief

When Rusty Westin went into the Owyhee Mountains a few weeks back, he was prepared for rain, cold, even loneliness.

What he hadn't counted on was a thief.

Westin had a friend drop him off on the Silver City road on a Friday. He left a ten-gallon water cooler hidden behind a rock pile, filled his canteen from the cooler, and hiked up to a ridge where he made camp.

When he hiked back down to get more water Saturday, the cooler had been stolen. His wife wasn't coming to get him until Monday evening.

Westin, who has spent a lot of time in the mountains, didn't panic without his water. He drank rainwater and water from a nearby stream that he boiled for tea. But he did find it disheartening that someone spending time in a remote area would steal another person's water.

The stolen cooler was one small indication of problems campers, hikers, and sportsmen are encountering in the mountains.

Westin knows that the time is past when folks can assume anything left out in the open will be safe. That's why he had someone drop him off. He didn't want to leave his car parked for three days.

"I used to leave a note on my car saying when I would be back, so people would know it wasn't abandoned," he says.

Now the note would be an open invitation to vandalism.

We all used to park our cars for a day hike or overnight camping trip without a thought. In camp, we'd put our food away but leave our tent and camp kitchen open while we went walking or fishing.

Cabins were left open too. Mountain etiquette dictated that a cabin be left unlocked for anyone caught in bad weather or without food.

Cabin courtesy dictated that anyone using the cabin leave it the same way he found it.

The same courtesy extended to abandoned cabins. My father once told me to put back a high button shoe I had found in an old cabin. The shoe, the old trunk I found it in, and the cabin were all part of a monument to the people who had lived there, my father explained. Taking the shoe was close to desecrating a grave.

I'm sure someone else took the shoe and the trunk with it. The cabin has probably been torn down for a subdivision.

We're losing more than cabins and coolers of water.

What's really disappearing is the trust we felt in the mountains, the calm assurance that, while nature might take a bite out of us, fellow travelers would not harm us.

Westin does not feel all is lost. He's noticed that some people are more courteous of others and of the mountains themselves than they were ten years ago.

Those people are on the right road. The only way to inspire trust is to extend it.

But, until everyone understands mountain etiquette, it's sadly best to lock everything or hide it away.

No Honor in Brazil

When I lived in Brazil twenty years ago, most of the houses in my neighborhood had two pictures on the mud walls—the Virgin Mary and John Kennedy.

Kennedy had a place of honor because the Brazilian people loved him. He was the president of a powerful foreign country, but he spoke to them and to their problems.

Late last week, another U.S. president was in Brazil. But I doubt President Bush's picture is going to find its way onto many Brazilian walls.

Bush went to Rio de Janeiro to attend the Earth Summit. Because he signed up at the last minute, his Secret Service agents had to stay in a motel that usually rents by the hour.

That wasn't our delegation's only laughable moment. Most of our country's performance at the conference was a deadly joke.

First the U.S. refused to sign a biodiversity treaty signed by every other major economic power.

Then we thwarted efforts by other countries to negotiate a treaty on global warming. Bush signed it, but only after seeing it was watered down.

We were picketed by fellow Americans disgusted by our delegation's actions and were criticized by some of the delegation's members.

Through it all, I couldn't help imagining the Brazilians I know listening to the summit news. I'll bet my last cruzeiro they were making cynical jokes.

These are the same people who have been hearing for years that the Americans want them to save their rainforest, protect their endangered species, preserve the way of life for Indian tribes living in the rainforest.

We're still sending them the same messages. But Bush's summit message is loud and clear: Don't make us sacrifice anything. You little guys do it.

The Brazilians shouldn't be surprised by our attitude. It was the same story twenty years ago.

The first time I went to the beach in my town, I was warned to wear thongs and take a towel I didn't care about ruining.

The sand looked clean. But one step into it and my sandals were covered with sticky tar. An off-shore oil rig had caught fire, spewing oil.

Brazilians and Americans were working the oil rig. After it blew, the Brazilians had to live with the mess.

At that time, the Amazon was opened up to homesteaders. People willing to clear the land and work it could claim it, the same way a lot of our families ended up with land in the West.

The homestead plan in the Amazon turned into an ecological disaster. But the former Brazilian president had a point when he told scolding Americans, "You had your chance to become rich. Now it's our turn."

Now the Brazilians and the Brazilian government recognize that they should protect what's left of the rainforest and the people and animals there.

When I went back to Brazil several years ago, people were wearing T-shirts saying: "We're doing away with the green in our flag." They talked to me with real concern about their damaged environment and ways to save it without destroying work for poor people.

Now they're watching their president sign the biological diversity treaty. And they're seeing our president refuse.

FRIENDS AND NEIGHBORS

A True Hero

Theresa de Kerpely died August 27, a few months after this column was written.

Heroes come in many sizes.

Some are huge and muscular, tough-talking guys who change the world by brute force. But one of my heroes is a diminutive and demure woman of ninety-four.

Theresa de Kerpely became larger than life for me nine years ago when I read *Of Love and Wars*, her last book of six. Her stirring and descriptive story begins with the birth of her first child in England during World War I and ends as she is starting her career as a published author in California during the late 1950s.

Between those bookends of new beginnings lies her haunting account of life in Budapest before and during World War II. The powerful scenes of beauty and devastation she paints will never leave me or anyone who has read *Of Love and Wars*.

Because of one chapter in that life, she is being recognized as a hero for a different reason. The state of Israel is honoring her for saving the life of Istvan Anhalt, a Jewish man, during World War II.

The story of Anhalt's rescue and shelter in the de Kerpely home is included in *Of Love and Wars*.

". . . I was very surprised to see, as I drew the blackout curtain over my window before putting on a light, a tall figure in the unmistakable garb of a Catholic priest walking up our street in the rapidly falling dusk of one of the shortest days in the year. Where could he be going at this dangerous hour—and for what reason? To my amazement, he stopped at our gate.

"It was Istvan, and this time he had come to stay."

The young man, a composer, had escaped from a labor company and been given the cassock and papers of a priest by the head of a monastery. And then he had turned to friends, the de Kerpelys, for shelter and protection.

After the war, Anhalt went to Paris to complete his music studies. In 1948, he immigrated to Canada where he became one of the country's foremost composers.

But he stayed in touch with Theresa de Kerpely, as she moved first to California, then to Boston and finally, in 1984, to Boise to be with her family. And he never forgot what the de Kerpelys had done for him.

Shortly after a visit to Israel, he nominated her for the Righteous Among The Nations Award.

"I feel very touched by the award," she says. "He has remained such a loyal friend. Gratitude is a rare virtue. People are apt to forget. He's never forgotten."

Righteous Among The Nations is the highest civil honor that can be bestowed on an individual by the state of Israel. Theresa de Kerpely was given the award April 2. Her name is listed in the Garden of the Righteous at Yad Vashem, Jerusalem, as a hero of the holocaust.

"One feels humble in the face of an award like that," she says.

Nevertheless, it is an honor that she richly deserves.

Hard Day

Willis Hovey just went through one of the hardest days he's ever had.

Two weeks ago, Hovey turned over the keys of Moon's Kitchen to the cafe's new owner and said good-bye to a job he didn't want to leave.

"It was one of the toughest things I've ever done," he says.

Arthritis, made worse by years of scooping hard ice cream for shakes, forced Hovey to give up Moon's. He sold it to Ransom Smith, who's learned how to make a Moon shake.

Hovey came back to Moon's recently to take care of last-minute business, say hello to friends, and have a cigarette and a cup of coffee at one of the tables he used to wait.

"I walk in here, everybody says, 'Hey,'" he says, throwing his arms wide. "It makes a big difference."

Moon's was Hovey's home for eleven years. He remembers the first day as clearly as the last.

The cafe had been closed for several years when Hovey bought it from Bernie Moon.

Then, as now, the cafe was in the back part of a gun and tackle store. Hovey stopped in for a special fish hook that the store carried. He remembers asking Bernie why he didn't sell the cafe to someone.

"He said, 'I can't find anybody with any guts,'" Hovey says, laughing. "I said, 'I'll be back Monday.' Monday, I had me a restaurant."

The first day in business, he took in twenty-two dollars.

"It was pretty scary. I remember it real well."

That was October, 1979.

One day in early 1982, Hovey started wondering if a good, old-fashioned shake would bring in more business.

"I grew up on milk shakes. I knew what they were supposed to taste like."

He bought some ice cream and some fruit and created the famous Moon shake.

The milk shakes brought in the families and the high school kids who knew how to mind their manners. The shakes also created a few scenes right out of a Charlie Chaplin movie.

"We called the first five stools at the counter the suicide zone," Hovey says. "One of those shakes would fly off the spinner and get all five of them."

But Moon's—with plenty to eat, friendly service, and a note on the cash register that says, "Checks cashed up to $20, six IDs and a $50 deposit required"—was never just a family place.

It brought in the businessmen and lawyers, the governors, judges, and legislators as well.

"I think half the bills that went through the House went through here," Hovey says. "Every time you approach the table with a coffeepot, everyone gets quiet. It's kind of comical."

He takes a last swig of coffee and looks around the place.

"A lot of times you leave a job and think, 'God, I'm tired of it.' I'd go to bed wishing I was getting up. I looked forward to coming down here."

Sun Valley Connection

If you don't want to know how the movie "Bugsy" ends, don't read this column.

In order to tell you about the Bugsy-Idaho connection, I'm going to have to reveal the end of the film and of Bugsy.

Bugsy Siegel, the mobster played by Warren Beatty in the movie, died violently. And he left Virginia Hill, his vamp girlfriend played by Annette Bening, to fend for herself. Which she did nicely by fleeing to Sun Valley.

Long-time Sun Valley residents Don and Gretchen Fraser remember Hill, although they didn't know her well.

"She kept to herself," Don Fraser says. "And we didn't want to mix with her too much. We didn't know exactly what was going on."

One thing they did know, along with other Sun Valley residents, was that Hill was getting financial support from somewhere. It was arriving weekly in shoe boxes.

"She did get money sent up to her, in cash, in shoe boxes," Don Fraser says.

People noticed that she paid for everything in one hundred dollar bills. Sometimes a lucky bellboy would take away a one hundred dollar tip.

Before long, she was attracting attention of another sort. Hans Hauser, an Austrian ski instructor with Clark Gable looks, fell in love with her.

Until he met Bugsy's former girlfriend, Hauser had been a happy bachelor.

"He was a big, handsome Austrian and a good skier," Fraser says. "All the gals went for the instructors and they really liked him."

Friends tried to tell Hauser he should forget Hill.

Otto Lang, one-time head of Sun Valley's ski school and later a movie producer, had a long conversation with Hauser about marriage with Hill.

"(I said) 'You'd be cutting yourself off from all your friends. . .'" Lang said in the book *Sun Valley* by Doug Oppenheimer and Jim Poore.

Lang thought he had talked Hauser out of marriage. The next day, he heard Hauser and Hill had eloped.

The couple moved to Spokane, Washington, where Hauser sold fire extinguishers.

"He didn't really have to work as long as those shoe boxes kept coming," Fraser says.

Still, married life was not easy for Hauser. Hill was questioned by the Kefauver Senate Committee over her connections with organized crime. Then questions over unpaid income tax came up. The couple fled to Austria.

"I think they were rather happy for a while there," Fraser says.

But the violence that had surrounded Hill's life caught up with them. Hill died from poisoning.

"The circumstances of her death were mysterious, whether she was poisoned or whether she took the poison herself," Fraser says.

And Hauser, the charming ski instructor with the dashing good looks, eventually hung himself.

A Family Team

For many of us, Mother's Day is one of the few days we get to share with our mothers and children. For Caryl Humphries and Dorothy Dutton, sharing is an everyday occurrence.

Caryl and her mother both take care of the Humphries' two small daughters. And the women also work together.

They began sharing lives when Caryl was pregnant with her first child. She and her mother started joking about Dorothy moving to Boise to help with her new grandchild.

Before long, the women and Caryl's husband, Ed, were seriously considering the idea. Dorothy moved here in July, 1990, just before her first granddaughter was born. The two families live next door to each other.

But the Mother's Day story doesn't end there.

Caryl, who is a teacher, wanted to take some time off after her baby was born. Her mother is a teacher with thirty-three years experience and a doctorate in reading.

Mother and daughter decided to share Caryl's fourth-grade class.

Dorothy taught for nine weeks while Caryl stayed home with her baby. Then Caryl went back to her classroom and Dorothy dropped in for special projects.

Sharing a job with Mom could be difficult or even impossible for a lot of people. But these two women, with their teaching experience and respect for each other, pulled it off.

"We have a similar style of teaching. Mom was my mentor," Caryl says. "At the time, Mom was living with us. We'd talk every night."

There's more to the story. The two women are now writing a fourth-grade book together, called *A Rendezvous with Idaho History*.

They started in the fall and have completed a rough draft. And they've managed to do it without any arguments. In fact, they actually sit down at the computer together to rewrite chapters.

"The main thing we had to do is give up ownership of it," Dorothy says. "It's ours. It's not, 'This is my chapter. Keep your hands off of it.'"

"If we're getting frustrated about something, we just talk about it," Caryl says. "I think we're so much alike that it helps."

Their work together is just an extension of the rest of their lives. They share everything with an ease that would amaze many people in this era of the dysfunctional family.

Dorothy admits she worried about being so much a part of her daughter's life when they first talked about it.

"I swore up and down I'd never do this to my children," she says. "But it's been really great watching those grandbabies."

Dorothy knows when to back out of her daughter's life, Caryl says.

"Sometimes I feel like I'm the one that nags," she adds with a laugh. "But it's been very nice . . . . I think Kelsey's going to be shocked when she realizes other kids' grandmothers don't live next door."

Knowing the President

A few days ago, somebody wondered aloud what Hillary Clinton will wear to the inaugural ball. I found myself wondering what dress I'll wear.

I'm not really going to the inaugural ball for the next president of the United States. I don't even know Bill and Hillary Clinton. But I feel like I do.

Part of that feeling comes from having them in the paper every morning and on television every night. But I've lived with other candidates this long and never felt like we were friends.

The difference is that I really do know the president-elect and his wife. I know their music. I can guess what they eat for snacks and how they divvy up their household chores. I know how they dance.

Because, no matter whether I agree with their political views or not, these people are like me. We were born within a few years of each other. We grew up together and were shaped by the same national events.

There are ways, of course, in which that doesn't matter at all. I've had presidents I loved, presidents I hated. But soon I'm going to have a president who's part of my generation.

I do believe that will make him a different kind of president than we've seen before.

It's already made a mark on the way we judge our candidates. As all of us in Clinton's generation watched him answer questions about marijuana and marital problems, we could only wriggle uncomfortably.

Very few of us went through those years without trying marijuana. A lot of us saw marriages come apart. We don't feel comfortable using those yardsticks to measure character. I doubt we'll hear those questions in the next campaign.

I think we're also rid of military service as the measure of a candidate's worth.

My friends and I did not all agree on whether the United States should be fighting in Vietnam. But we lived directly with the questions it raised and its consequences.

I was a young wife then, growing fearful that my husband would be drafted to fight in a war I thought was insane. I saw one friend go to Canada, sat through the memorial service of another who died a horrible death in the rice paddies, saw another come back from the war so damaged emotionally that he never recovered.

We came through those years understanding the men who decided not to go to Vietnam as well as those who went.

We fought other battles—for civil rights, for women's rights, for changes in a government we felt was corrupt. We were involved in campus and urban riots. We saw one president assassinated, another nearly impeached.

We learned to question the way things were done. We discovered that we could be against government policy and still be for our democracy. We learned that we had the power to make changes.

Like all of us in our forties, Bill and Hillary Clinton have beliefs that were forged by the fires of our times. Bill Clinton's presidency will reflect our common history.

In one way or another, we will be in the Clinton White House. Even if we aren't invited to the inaugural ball.

Men Hugging

This column was written the day of President Clinton's inauguration.

What can you say about a president's inaugural parade that includes the Precision Lawnchair Demonstration Team?

Only one thing—the baby boomers are in charge.

Whether you love him or wish you could leave him, you have to admit that President Bill Clinton is a flag-waving member of his generation.

The crackerjack lawnchair team proves our forty-six-year-old president has hung onto the sophisticated sense of humor we in his generation developed in our youth.

But the lawnchair snappers, fascinating as they are, weren't the only indication that one of us has taken over.

There was the music, of course. Judy Collins, Bob Dylan, Aretha Franklin. What other president could sing along with the Queen of Soul and not miss a word of "Respect." What other president, for that matter, could reunite a rock group like Fleetwood Mac.

It'll be a long time before I forget the sight of a group of Sikhs, dressed in their long white robes and turbans, rocking to the beat of "Don't Stop (Thinking About Tomorrow)."

We may not see that again, but we're definitely going to be seeing another mark of our generation—hugs among men. Try to imagine Ike and Nixon or Reagan and Bush in a clinch. But Clinton and Vice-President Al Gore gave each other a big bear hug after Gore was sworn in.

In fact, they've been falling into each other's arms quite regularly in the past few months. I predict the trend will spread as male members of other generations attempt to prove they're part of the "in" crowd.

Once they've learned how to touch without flinching, older guys are going to take up jogging.

I know, I know. Bush took the press corps for a few sprints. But this week we were treated to the sight of a president in serious sweats running serious miles with a gang of friends.

And, like most of us in the exercise generation, Clinton combines his dedication to vigorous workouts with a passion for junk food.

Reagan had his jelly beans, Bush his pork rinds. But nobody can hope to compete with a member of the first generation that grew up on fast food.

After the swearing-in ceremony, Clinton did eat a tasteful lunch that included broccoli.

But, as I saluted him with one of his own peanut butter and banana sandwiches, I knew his heart wasn't in that lunch. I bet as soon as the cameras were off him, he sneaked off for a greasy cheeseburger with all the trimmings.

Any of us would have done the same thing.

Spreading Kindness

If you can't stand happiness, beware. Random acts of kindness are spreading.

A while ago, I wrote about people throughout the country who are giving and receiving moments of kindness that weren't requested and may go unrewarded.

The stories came from a book called *Random Acts of Kindness.* In *Random Acts*, counselor Dawna Markova says, "Giving in this way is as effective as an anti-depressant."

Many readers understood Markova's words. After I wrote about *Random Acts*, they were willing to share their own experiences.

One woman wrote about losing her husband, home, financial security, many friends and "just about my last shred of sanity."

She ended up in an institution in another state.

"I had been there about a month when I got a call from a woman I had known in better days. After a long search, she had found me and wanted to come visit. I was horrified. This person was familiar with me as a successful, independent woman. I gave her a flat no.

"You don't know what you'll see here," I said. "This place is full of crazy people, street people, criminal people. And I'm one of them. You don't know what you'll see."

" 'No' she said, 'but I know you.' "

"The fact that one person saw beyond my outward circumstances to see me . . . still brings tears to my eyes. She had faith in me when I couldn't have faith in myself."

Another woman wrote about the family barn burning down a few days before Christmas. One neighbor caught their runaway horse that was headed for rush hour traffic, then offered to board it. Friends came and took the family's children home, "fed them dinner and kept them until the fire was out."

A second neighbor brought over a load of hay the next morning to feed the horses. Another neighbor prepared and leveled the ground when it was time to rebuild the barn.

". . . when we tried to pay him, he told us to repay him by helping someone else in their time of need."

Finally, a reader wrote about having to take a train home when she was ill and in pain.

". . . my sister and her husband took me to the train, and she got on with me to help me find a seat. There was none; soldiers filled every seat and stood in the aisle. Then the train started, and my sister was caught, couldn't get off, and I was still jammed in the aisle. I started sobbing. Beside us six soldiers sat in facing seats meant for four. Three of those blessed soldiers got up, gave us their seats, and they stood the rest of the journey.

"Angels come in all guises. Those wore uniforms."

Gentle Tio

For most of us, Cesar Chavez is a heroic figure, a man larger than life who fought the big boys to win rights for the members of his United Farm Workers.

But for Carmen Gonzales, Chavez was "tio." Gonzales, who now lives in Boise, grew up in Delano, California, near the Chavez' house. Chavez was not a blood uncle of Gonzales. But, as a little girl, she played with the younger Chavez children and was in and out of their house.

"When he gave you a cookie, whatever, he always had a smile," Gonzales says. "His face was always so kind and gentle. And his eyes were sad. You could tell he'd felt anguish and pain. A little child doesn't know those words, but you could see it."

Gonzales knew something else about her tio as well. For her parents, Chavez was a special person.

"All I knew was that he was a helper. I didn't understand, but I knew my parents respected him."

Gonzales was one of fourteen children. Her father worked on the railroad, in the fields, at odd jobs, "whatever he could do to keep us fed." Her mother, she says, never ventured out of the house.

But Gonzales, at age six or seven, was allowed to go into the fields under the watchful eye of her godmother. It was among these field workers that Chavez brought his message of a better life and the strikes that would be necessary to win workers' rights.

"In the beginning, there was a lot of confusion," Gonzales says of that time.

"All these people had known was to do what they were told. No matter how you feel, or if your kids are sick or whatever, you go or you lose the very little you have. All they'd known in their lives was working in those fields."

When Chavez and the farm workers began organizing and then striking, Gonzales and other children went door-to-door, passing out pamphlets and telling people about meetings.

And she recalls vividly a confrontation on her street between striking workers and a neighbor who was loading watermelons for one of the ranches.

"I was out in the yard playing," she says. "People started walking toward this guy's house with bats and broomsticks. They started throwing watermelons off the trucks. I just stood there shocked. I knew all these people. It was neighbor against neighbor."

Eventually, the United Farm Workers union grew strong enough to stage a nationwide boycott of table grapes. In 1970, the union signed contracts with the main Delano growers.

Gonzales left Delano and went on to a college education and another life in Boise. But she hasn't forgotten the place where she grew up.

"That upbringing gives me an advantage," she says. "I know what it's like on both sides of the fence."

And she hasn't forgotten her tio, a gentle hero with a ready smile for a little girl.

Mail Tales

Dear Ann Landers: I've been reading all of the recent gripes in your column about the post office, and I just had to write.

I know people have bad things happen to their mail. They've been telling you about lost letters, late letters, and other laments.

I understand their whining. Before I moved to Boise, I had mail woes that would make you weep.

But now I am a happy mailer. When I pass my mail carrier on the street, we wave. When I go to my post office, I am greeted with smiles. My mail goes out, my mail comes in. It's on time and it's my mail.

The people in the Boise P.O. not only know how to get my mail to me—they go the extra mile.

When we moved to a new house, we had to perch our mail box on top of a tall pole until a curb could be poured and the pole sunk. Our postal carrier, not a large woman, must have made flying leaps to hit our box. But we always had our mail.

The folks in our neighborhood post office are the same way. They've given me tape for my packages and advice for sending things the cheapest way.

When I was there the other day, one of them was selling large envelopes to the woman in front of me.

"If you don't use them, you can bring them back," she told her.

When I got up to the counter, I noticed a small sign attached to the electronic meter that reads out mailing costs. The sign joked, "Now are you completely depressed?"

These people seem to be enjoying their work. They kid around with each other and the customers without slowing down the line. Even at Christmas, Ann, it's a cheery place.

I know I sound like a postal Pollyanna. But I do remember the bad old days, when I wondered if my mail was going to a post office or a garbage dump.

My parents and I lived for a time in your fair city of Chicago. We affectionately called the post office "the black hole." It wasn't a question of courteous service. It was a question of any service at all.

My parents once received a package, several months late, that had been found frozen in ice in the bottom of a mail truck.

After I moved to Boise, I received a Christmas card from a friend still in Chicago. From the letter and pictures enclosed, I decided her children were moving backwards in time. They were smaller and in lower grades than the last time I'd seen them.

I called her.

"What card?" she said and then paused. "I mailed that to you two years ago."

If I'd still been living in Chicago, I would have guessed. But being in Boise has spoiled me.

Ann, one of your letter writers said that his mother had mailed a letter to him in Italy and attached two quarters instead of stamps. When he got the letter, it still had the quarters taped on the envelope.

If it had been my post office, they would have stuck the stamps on for me and made sure I got the change.

Pantyhose War

Just when you think elected officials don't understand how the rest of us live, Lydia Justice Edwards writes to Ralph Nader about women's hose.

That's right. Our state treasurer has pulled up her socks and taken up the cry for an end to hosiery discrimination against women.

What she is calling for is a pair of hose that won't run the first time you wear them.

As she says in her letter to Nader, "You would have the undying gratitude of millions of women who have enough frustrations in life without watching their last pair of pantyhose—fresh from the package—create ladder-like runners up their legs as they rush to dress for work."

Okay, okay. We all know that ripped, snagged hose are not at the top of the troubles list for a lot of people. But they're more than an annoyance for women required to wear them every day on the job.

As Edwards points out, they're also big bucks.

Like any good treasurer, she's kept accurate records of the numbers. And they're not pretty.

After Edwards decided to confront the hosiery industry on its shoddy product, she saved all her ruined pantyhose for one year. At the end of the year, she had a pile with 130 pairs.

"At an average of $4 per pair, that's an expenditure of $520," she writes.

But she didn't stop there. She did a little checking in the men's sock department.

"Men's stockings, by comparison, cost an average of $6.50 (very generous figure) and I estimate annual purchase at twenty-four pairs (again, very generous estimate). Total cost, based on these figures is $156."

That's a difference of $364 a year.

Edwards goes on to discuss what every woman knows in her heart. If they really wanted to, hosiery companies could come up with a product that would look good and wear well.

"This is a cruel joke being played on American women and is the lowest form of discrimination—it penalizes by costing more for those who earn less because of other forms of discrimination," she writes.

Edwards didn't just send her complaint to Nader. She wrote to Hanes Hosiery, the company whose pantyhose she buys.

Hanes replied with a letter that said, in part, "We regret you have experienced a problem with one of our products. . ."

The letter, which sounds a lot like the usual form letter sent to any customer who complains, went on to say that Hanes had experimented with a run-proof knit, but "the garment had a thick and unappealing appearance."

Edwards' response to Hanes is basically, "Uh-huh, sure."

"Hanes' reply letter does not satisfy my inquiry," she wrote to Nader, "and I really don't think it's the caliber of letter which merits my response."

Nader is calling for the American public to let him know about our own hosiery horror stories.

If enough of us complain, we could bring an end to a frustration that's costing us money. We might even put Idaho on the map for more than potatoes.

Son of Pantyhose

The stocking saga marches on.

State Treasurer Lydia Justice Edwards is doing battle against pricey hose that run before you can say "planned obsolescence." After writing to Ralph Nader, she started hearing from women tired of ladders up their legs.

"As I travel and speak, people don't ask me about taxes now," she says. "They say, 'I'm so glad you're doing something about pantyhose.'"

She has received half a dozen letters cheering her on and imparting fresh hosiery stories.

One letter writer enclosed a pair of hose made in the '50s that haven't worn out. Edwards even had a call from the U.S. Coast Guard on the subject.

"I wondered why in the world the Coast Guard would be calling me," she says.

It turns out one of the Coast Guard men sells pantyhose for a company called Sheer Magic.

"He wanted to send me some. He asked me to give him my dimensions."

Edward received four pair of Sheer Magic pantyhose and distributed them to her staff for a test drive. She also is contacting the Federal Trade Commission to look into the high prices of hosiery and cosmetics.

"I'm very serious about this," she says. "This is not a lark."

Niels Young, who lives in Boise, read about Edwards' quest and decided to write to Nader about the male side of the issue.

It seems that Young used to buy nylon socks that were guaranteed for five years and really lasted that long. But, like other good things, the Camp Fisherman Knit socks disappeared from the market.

"I am disgusted at what appears to be a greedy and short range attitude that would lead to such a corporate decision!" Young wrote.

A representative from the Camp Hosiery Company called Young and explained that sales on the nylon sock had dropped off. Cotton socks, he said, sell better.

Young wasn't convinced by the arguments but he was heartened to hear that the company still had twenty dozen pair of the Fisherman Knit socks in stock. Would Young like to buy them at cost?

He decided to take ten dozen pair, a more than lifetime supply. Alas, his short-lived sock hopes were dashed. It turned out the computer showed twenty dozen pair in the warehouse but, in fact, the cupboard was bare.

So now Young is left with a choice—to sock badly or not to sock?

He is looking to the example of the late, great Albert Einstein. The genius, Young says, wore no socks.

"I may," says Young, "do an Albert Einstein."

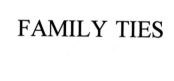

FAMILY TIES

Life Lesson

The pain started at 5:30 on a Friday night. By 6, my husband knew he needed help. By 6:30, the emergency room staff knew they were looking at a bad gallbladder with complications.

We didn't know it, but we were looking at an eight-day hospital stay. I say "we" and that's exactly what I mean. My husband was the patient. But when someone you love is sick and in pain, your world narrows down to his pain.

Until last week, I didn't understand that. I've always been the person in the bed. My husband had confined his hospital experience to visiting my room.

He was about to learn what it means to be a patient. I was about to learn what it's like to be the well one.

Easy, I'd always thought. You sit by the sickbed, looking like Julia Roberts in "Dying Young." Then, your husband stands up, declares himself well and the two of you slow-mo into the sunset.

Life, unfortunately, does not always imitate art. But, like the best books and films show us, there are lessons to be learned from painful, even scary, times.

I first learned that most of my daily life was not important.

It didn't matter if the weeds in the yard grew a foot high, which they did. It didn't matter whether the dishes were washed or the bed made. I didn't care what I looked like, what I ate.

What I cared about, intensely, were the events happening to my husband in Room 410.

Things I'd never even heard of before, like amylase levels (used to check the progress of the pancreas), made me jubilant or depressed. The way my husband was being taken care of by the nurses and doctors—and they were wonderful—was my focus.

Most of my suddenly former life went on without me. The pieces that didn't were taken care of by family and friends. I learned that I could ask them for help, something I'm not that good at, and it was okay.

Two friends stopped their busy lives to come and sit with me when I realized at the last minute that I didn't want to be alone during my husband's surgery. Another friend listened to my long list of worries when she didn't really have a minute to spare.

A neighbor made sure I could ignore our irrigation system for a week when I confessed I didn't have a clue about moving the gates.

Family checked in every day, comforting me and offering to come at any time. Other friends dropped by, called, sent flowers and cards, said they would do anything they could and meant it.

Life was pared down to a room, the illness of the person I care about most in the world, and the people who cared enough about us to be there when we needed them.

The crisis is over. My husband is home and recuperating. My life is getting back to normal, which means filling up fast with the duties we call living.

I'm glad the days in Room 410 are over. But I hope I never forget what they taught me. It's easy to spend all your time on weeds that need to be pulled. It's more important to stop and smell the flowers.

Bad News

The letter was not unexpected. But it still made me sad.

"G. and I decided to get a friendly divorce."

That explained why we hadn't heard from them for too many months, why we hadn't received a Christmas package from them. Somehow I knew that eventually we would hear from them and the news wouldn't be good.

The last time we'd been together for a vacation, they seemed like they were growing apart.

Still, despite having a sense that something was going wrong, I didn't want this to happen. How could they do this to us? We were going to grow old together.

We started out young together.

They got married the same year we did. We went to their wedding, spent most of our weekends with them, shared big trips when we had money and food when we didn't.

When we moved away, they got our table and our promise that we would be back.

We were. Despite being half a world away, we got together as often as we could. It was always as though we'd never been apart.

Now we'll never be together again.

We'll see them, of course. We'll see her, in her new apartment, maybe in her new town. We'll see him, maybe with a new wife. It will be pleasant. It might even be fun. But it won't be the same.

When you share a history with someone, there's a lot that doesn't have to be said. Old stories don't have to be explained, old jokes don't have to be retold.

Now some jokes won't make sense to new people in their lives. And some stories will be painful instead of funny. Our friendship, our common history, will go through a little death, just as their marriage has.

Why did I think this wouldn't happen to us? The statistics told me it would. My own experience with an early marriage and divorce should have left me feeling, "This can happen to anybody."

Instead, after marrying again, I thought all my friends would be like us and beat the odds.

We would be the group who never had heartache or illness, never died, never split up.

When the first pair of friends decided to throw in the towel, I was devastated. I decided to save myself from more heartbreak by figuring out which friends wouldn't make it. Six divorces later, I know there's no way to tell.

Of the four couples we were friends with in the early days of our marriage, three have split up.

The fourth I wouldn't have given six months. My mother, after having dinner at their house, thought they weren't going to make it through the evening.

They stayed together. Everyone else is now divorced. And we're left wondering, once again, who will be our traveling companions through life.

Taking the Time

Like fourteen million other people, I watched parts of "The Civil War" on television.

People planned their evenings around the documentary, discussed it at work the next day. We talked about battles with real men instead of numbers, generals made human, lives that were cut off or changed forever.

We learned what it was like to live through the war or die in it.

The people, so often missing in historical accounts, came alive through haunting photographs and through their poignant letters and diaries.

We discussed those letters in our "morning-after" sessions. They were so beautifully written that they sounded like poetry. It didn't seem possible that ordinary soldiers could have written so eloquently.

But they could and they did.

The language they used is still in our vocabulary today. We could be as eloquent as the soldier who wrote to his wife, "If there be a soft breeze upon your cheek, it shall be my breath . . . my spirit passing by."

We have the same feelings those people had. We are as educated as most of them were. We could write letters like theirs. But we think we don't have the time.

It does take time to write a letter. You have to think about what you want say, how you want to say it.

You have to choose your words carefully because they will stay on the page. They won't disappear into the air like a phone call. They won't be tossed into the wastebasket like a computer printout.

They will last, a small piece of history to be handed down.

It's only been recently that we've forgotten the value of letters. Our parents and our grandparents knew how to share a day and a piece of themselves with their families through letters.

When my mother was learning to write letters, her father, a kind man, would not let her scribble. Letters, he said, are too important. They deserve your best handwriting.

He and my grandmother wrote letters every Sunday evening.

I still have most of the letters my grandmother wrote to me. Looking at her letters, seeing her handwriting, I see her.

Reading her thoughts, written in the elegant rounded style of Spencerian handwriting, I hear her voice and feel as if she's right there with me.

We think it takes too much time to write a letter by hand these days. We need to get information out and get it out fast. We have to phone it out, fax it out, get on to the next letter.

We hurry through the lists of information and forget that there are people behind the facts, thoughts and emotions behind the events.

If the men and women who lived through the Civil War had hurried through their letters and limited their writing to lists of information and events, we would never have known them.

And we would have been the poorer for it.

Good-bye to a Friend

The call came in the middle of the night. It was bad news.

Carmelia, the friend I lived with during my last stay in Brazil, was dead. She had gone in for a routine operation. During surgery, her heart stopped.

It's been several days since that chilling call. I still can't grasp that Carmelia is gone. It doesn't seem possible that someone so full of life is not here anymore.

Carmelia stepped into my life twenty-three years ago as a lively Peace Corps instructor from Brazil.

Younger than all of the Peace Corps trainees, she soon became our mentor. While we were shaking in our sandals, wondering if we would live through stateside training, she was jumping joyfully into her first visit to America.

Once we got back to Brazil, she continued the lessons on language and life.

She introduced me to her large family who took me in like the lost child I was. She showed me where to buy the best food in the market, how to use it in a good Brazilian dish, and where to eat out if it didn't work.

She gently corrected my wavering Portuguese, then gave me some great slang words so I wouldn't sound like a language tape.

She told me, after a good belly laugh, why my exact translation of "the car is being serviced" left my landlord thinking the Peace Corps jeep was using the bathroom.

She explained the inner workings of her culture to me, even when it meant giving me "subversive" information in those days of a repressive military government.

She was one of the most intelligent people I've ever known. But she never let it go to her head.

Because she was small, some of her friends called her "Baixinha" or "little short one." After she received her Ph.D. from Georgetown University, a friend called her "Baixinha." She drew herself up to her full four-foot-ten and said, "That's Doctor Baixinha."

She loved a funny story, even on herself. When I was living with her, she told me the little boy next door kept trying to come over and play because he thought they were the same age.

One day, he told his father he was going to drive the car. His father said, "You're too young."

"But," the boy replied, "the little girl next door does."

She gave me more than humorous stories when I lived with her. She introduced me to all her friends, some new naughty Portuguese phrases, and a soap opera that hooked us both.

She lent me her house, her family, her support. When I left, she lent me a suitcase for all my souvenirs.

The best souvenir is my memory of that time together.

That will never leave me. But she has been taken away. I feel sad, bewildered, robbed of all the future we were going to have together.

She was a guide through my world. Without her, I'm a little lost.

Pals

I have good news for all you parents trying to pry apart fighting children. My brother is one of my friends.

It was not always so. There were times, I'm sure, when my parents must have wondered if the two kids would live to adulthood. Scar tissue was not even questioned.

Like siblings everywhere, we took out physical energy on each other's bodies. We learned, as only family members can, where the psychological soft spots were as well.

On rainy days, we picked on each other out of boredom. On sunny days, we competed indoors and out for our parents' attention.

The rivalry started the day they brought my brother home from the hospital. I took a couple of looks in the basket and then went out to tell the neighbors about my cool new trike.

A short time later, I tried to fold up his playpen with him in it.

As soon as he got beyond the baby stage, he began to fight back. But, in between the squabbles, we started playing together.

We rigged up a rope in a tree and took turns leaping into our creek. We bellied through the grass on the plateau overlooking the creek, keeping our heads down in case of enemies. We conquered mountains the size of molehills and thought we were heroes.

I still had time to torment my brother. But let anyone else start in on him and, in the best older sibling tradition, I would defend him violently.

As we got older, he didn't need me as much. I needed him, though, as a way back into childhood.

With my girlfriends, I had to be grown up, wear lipstick and talk about boys. With my brother and his friends, I could be a kid, playing kick-the-can and ice hockey.

When I left home for college, we seemed to grow apart. We still cared about each other; we just didn't see each other much.

I graduated, he went to college. I went to South America, he went to Alaska.

A few years later, we reconnected and I found a friend.

We share a history. We grew up with the same parents, lived in the same neighborhoods, went to the same schools, had some of the same friends.

We may remember different parts of the same experience, but we had those experiences together.

We speak the same language. And there are things we never have to say in order to understand each other.

It's comforting to be with someone who's known you most or all of your life, who knows every one of your faults and still accepts and loves you.

Not every child is going to grow up being best friends with his brothers and sisters. Some siblings grow apart and stay apart. Some siblings don't deserve to be called a friend. Some families need to separate.

But, for many of us, our brothers and sisters are a way for us to feel truly home again.

ABOUT THE AUTHOR

Judy McConnell Steele has written a personal column for fifteen years. She grew up in Denver, Colorado, and remembers when it was a town like Boise. When not contemplating the world for her writing, she spends time with her husband, family, and friends. She loves to travel, but always comes back home.